A Street that Rhymed at 3am

MARK TIMLIN

A Street that Rhymed at 3am

VICTOR GOLLANCZ

LONDON

First published in Great Britain 1997
by Victor Gollancz
An imprint of the Cassell Group
Wellington House, 125 Strand, London WC2R 0BB

© Mark Timlin 1997

The right of Mark Timlin to be identified as author of
this work has been asserted by him in accordance with
the Copyright, Designs and Patents Act, 1988.

A catalogue record for this book is
available from the British Library.

ISBN 0 575 06405 6

Typeset by CentraCet, Cambridge
Printed in Great Britain by
St Edmundsbury Press Ltd, Bury St Edmunds, Suffolk

97 98 99 5 4 3 2 1

for Charlotte and Amy

'We deal in lead, friend'

Steve McQueen in
The Magnificent Seven

PROLOGUE

When the lift arrived in the deserted basement garage, we walked across the rubber- and oil-stained floor, looking for Latimer's car. Finally I spotted it in one corner and said, 'There it is, the blue saloon.'

Lopez just grunted in reply. I wasn't looking forward to sitting in any traffic jams with him. What the fuck am I doing here? I thought.

I got out the keys and walked round to the boot, when I heard a faint sound from the shadows, close to the gap where a dim sign proclaimed 'EXIT' in blue neon letters, and the back window of the SAAB imploded: another bullet screeched off the bodywork close to where I was standing, and Lopez, with an amazed look on his face, dropped the bag and coat he was carrying and fell to the ground with a thud. I saw muzzle flashes come from the darkness, but heard only the discreet coughs of silenced gun barrels.

I just stood there for a stunned second before reacting. Then I dropped the bag I was carrying too, ducked down behind the car and peered over the top of the boot.

Lopez was lying a yard or so away from me, scrabbling at the concrete with hands and feet. 'Help me!' he cried gutturally. 'For Christ's sake, help me!'

I had no choice. Risking more bullets, I crabbed away from the car on my hands and knees until I was next to him. I grabbed him by the collar of his jacket and his belt and dragged him awkwardly into the shelter of one of the buttresses that stuck out into the body of the car park. 'Oh shit!' he cried. 'Oh shit, oh fuck, oh Jesus Christ it hurts!'

7

It looked like it did too. The bullet had hit him dead in the centre of his back and exited through the front of his coat. There was blood spurting from both the entry and exit wounds. I tore off my jacket, ripped off my shirt and made a pad for his chest where most of the blood seemed to be coming from. 'Give me your hand,' I said.

He held up his hand and I placed it over the hole where the bullet had exited him and I pushed his palm hard against the flow of blood. 'Hold that tight,' I said.

'Oh Jesus!' he cried. 'Sweet Jesus help me!'

'Gun!' I screamed. 'Where's your fucking gun?'

'Jesus please . . .'

'The fucking gun!' I yelled, running my hands under his arm where he'd concealed it before, but felt nothing. Where the fuck did he keep the sodding thing? Or had he left it behind with Shapiro before getting ready for the flight? 'Lopez,' I almost screamed in a whisper. 'Are you armed?'

He stopped calling for divine intervention for a second and pointed with his free hand to his waist. I ran my hands round his belt and felt a concealed holster inside his trousers at the small of his back. I yanked up his jacket and pulled out his .45 automatic. The pistol was huge and heavy, warm from his body heat, and fitted into my hand like it had been custom-made for me. I chambered a round and held the gun in front of me. I heard a sound like a shoe scraping on concrete from behind a parked car and fired, spraying bullets every which way. I heard them clanging on to metal and smashing glass and hoped I didn't hit a fuel tank, or else detective kebab would be on the menu. I also hoped that it wasn't some innocent passer-by investigating the sound of the ambusher's bullets or I might be guilty of sending some civilian to an early grave. Before the clip was empty, I eased my finger off the trigger. I didn't have any spare magazines.

'Mother!' Lopez cried. 'Where are you?'

'She's not here,' I said. 'Shut up.'

'I can see her. Mother!' And he reached out the hand that wasn't pressed to his chest.

'No,' I said.

Then he turned and looked at me. 'Hold me,' he said. 'Hold me, Mother.'

Shit! I thought. He thinks I'm his fucking mum now. Under other circumstances it would've been hysterical. But here, now, it was as sad as shit.

I wiped a bloodstained hand across my face and went closer. I sat with my back against the brick and heaved him to me. He lay across my legs with his back against my chest, and the only thing I could think was that if the gunnie came round the corner, the first bullets would probably finish Lopez off. I held the gun straight out over his shoulder and waited.

'Oh Jesus fuck! Oh fuck, oh fuck, oh God, stop it hurting. Mother, help me!' He wouldn't stop.

I looked down at him and knew he was going fast. 'Momma. Momma. I said we'd be together some day.' He looked up. 'Momma,' he said. 'You look so beautiful.'

I touched his head. 'Don't worry,' I said. 'It'll be all right soon.' There was nothing I could do to help.

'Kiss me, Momma,' he said. 'Give me a kiss.'

I felt like someone was playing a cruel trick on us both.

'Kiss me,' he pleaded.

So I did. I leaned my head forward and gently touched his forehead with my lips. And as I did it, I felt the life ebb out of him and he slumped in my arms.

1

Friday night/Saturday morning

Judith was with me when it happened, thank God. Well, not with me exactly, and thank God for that too. See, she's fifteen now, a young woman. And I still live in the same little studio flat in Tulse Hill. And somehow it just didn't seem right any more for us to share a room. She never said a word, but she needs her privacy. And I do too. So when she comes to visit me, she stays round my mate Charlie's gaff. He's a car dealer and garage owner with a proper wife and two daughters of his own. And he's got a big house in West Norwood with lots of space and it's just a few minutes' drive away. Judith's always got on well with Charlie and his family, and vice versa, so all in all it worked out for the best.

Then one day, just over a week before Christmas, the best became the worst and would never be the same again.

The reason that Judith was down in London was that my ex-wife Laura and her new – well not so new now – husband Louis, and their son David were in America. Louis is a dentist and there was some sort of convention in New York. Then they were due to fly to Chicago, where Louis had a whole bunch of relatives, and spend the holiday there, with Judith meeting them the Tuesday before Christmas Day, which that year fell on a Monday. Now it was really my turn to have her for Christmas, but it was an opportunity she didn't want to miss, and I was quite happy to have her the week prior to her leaving and for a few more days when they all came back in the new year.

At the time I was doing some security work for a supermarket firm. No. Not dressed up in some pathetic imitation of an American cop's uniform with a radio on my hip and about as much authority as a spam salesman. I was undercover in the main warehouse, which was big enough to take half a dozen jumbo jets and was losing stock like a leaky sieve. That is if all sieves weren't leaky by definition. It had taken me a week and a half to work out who was at it. A right nasty little firm with one of the under-managers as the Mr Big. But proving it was a different matter, and on the day that Judith arrived from Aberdeen, I dumped what I'd found on the security director's desk and told him I didn't do the Christmas shift.

So there we were. The Friday night before Judith was due to jet out to Chicago. I'd taken her out for a Chinese in Streatham, then round to my local bar. Judith had tarted herself up so that she looked like twenty and I think most of the patrons in the place thought that I'd done a bit of cradle-snatching and was out with a new bird.

We'd sat in the bar till closing, me drinking JDs and Judith on the orange juice, having a great time taking the piss out of all and sundry. Then I'd walked her round to Charlie's, had a quick cuppa, then sloped off home and into bed, which is where I was when my phone rang at God knows what hour.

It was ten past three, as it happens, and I climbed out of a bad dream and into a worse one.

'Hello,' I said, when I'd remembered in my dazed state where the phone was.

'May I speak with Mr Nicholas Sharman?' a male voice with an American accent said.

'Speaking.'

'Mr Sharman. My name is Jake Kowalski. I am assistant chief of security at O'Hare Airport in Chicago.'

A freezing hand clutched at my gut.

'I am trying to trace the next of kin of Mrs Laura Rudnick.'

Rudnick was Louis's surname.

'I don't understand,' I said. 'Her husband is her next of kin.'

But I did understand. I just didn't want to admit it.

'Mr Sharman. Two hours ago, six o'clock in the evening our time, a Seagram International 747 incoming from New York City crashed on landing at the field.' His voice cracked. 'I'm afraid all four hundred passengers on board were killed. Mr and Mrs Rudnick and their son David were on the passenger manifest. We checked with the travel agency involved. A Ms Judith Sharman was listed as Mrs Rudnick's NOK in the event of an accident to the party. It was noted that she was a minor and could be contacted through you at this number. I'm so sorry, Mr Sharman. This place is mayhem. The holiday season and all. The airport has been closed and we've got flights stacked up from here to Alaska. I'm supposed to be off myself . . . But I don't expect you want to hear this.'

I didn't, but I felt for the geezer. His worst nightmare had just happened. 'Jesus,' I said. 'There's no chance of a mistake? A missed flight. Something like that.'

'They checked in an hour before take-off in New York. I'm sorry. I don't think there's a mistake at all.'

'What about Louis's family? They're in Chicago some-where.'

'Contact has been made. But they wanted us to get in touch with . . .' He hesitated, '. . . Judith and her guardian. I guess she's an orphan now.'

'Not while I'm still breathing. I'm her natural father.'

13

'Apologies, Mr Sharman. After twenty-five years in this business you never get used to this sort of situation.'

'Forget it,' I said. 'What arrangements are you making?'

'They're sketchy at the moment. To be blunt, the plane's hardly cool even though it's twenty below out here. Christ knows what state the bodies will be in . . .' Another pause. '. . . Sorry again.'

'I understand,' I said. 'I used to be a cop myself.'

'Thank God for that. Can I leave telling your daughter to you?'

'Of course.'

'I don't envy you.'

'I wouldn't envy you in the same circumstances.'

He gave me a number to contact and several names in case he was off duty. 'I'm so goddamn sorry it had to be done like this,' he said when I'd written them down. 'Anything we can do at O'Hare will be done.'

'It's not your fault.'

'But I'm the messenger. And you know what used to happen to the messengers who brought bad news.' He didn't wait for an answer. 'Well, so long, Mr Sharman, and a merr . . . Shit. Force of habit. It's not going to be, is it?'

'Not for me and my daughter,' I said, and broke the connection.

14

2

I dropped the phone beside me and lay back on the pillow as a wave of unutterable grief swept over me. 'Fuck,' I said aloud. 'Fuck, fuck, fuck.'

I looked at my watch. It was three-fifteen. Barely five minutes had passed since the phone rang and changed Judith's and my life for ever. And how many other lives would be changed before the day was much older? Hundreds, probably thousands, and all because a huge tube of pressurized air and frail humanity had somehow malfunctioned in a cold land thousands of miles away. Malfunctioned. Now there's a word.

I got up then, pulled on my dressing gown, went to the kitchenette and put on the kettle. As I heard the water inside begin to boil, I found a bottle of Jack in the kitchen cabinet and took a swig straight from the neck. As the raw liquor burnt its way down into my gut I saluted thin air with the bottle and said, 'Well, Stanley. Another fine mess you've got me into.'

I put down the bottle, stuck a teabag, milk and sugar into a cup, and when the kettle clicked off I added boiling water and stirred the contents round until I was satisfied with its strength.

I took the tea back to bed, found my cigarettes and lit one. It tasted bad. The tea didn't taste much better.

Laura, I thought. Jesus. Laura. If only I'd been a better man she would never have been flying over that frozen landscape. How did it feel? I wondered. Did they have time to realize what was happening? Did she hold Louis's hand as the plane dropped out of the sky? Did she manage to embrace her baby son who should've been mine, if only I'd been a better man?

15

Did she scream as the plane hit and burst into flames? Did she think of Judith? Did she think of me?

I tasted the tea again, lit another cigarette and looked at my watch. Three-thirty. Wasn't there news on the half-hour through the night on Channel 3?

I found the remote on the bed and hit the 'ON' button. The TV picture showed Big Ben then went to the news reader. The plane crash was the top story. With pictures. Normally you take that sort of thing for granted. Wars, famine, disaster brought to your home every hour on the half-hour, and you carry on snogging your girlfriend or eating a slice of pizza. Unless it's a picture of one of the few people you've ever loved being barbecued for the edification of the nation. Then you switch off and, try as you might not, begin to cry.

Then the phone rang again.

I picked it up. 'Hello,' I said with a gulp, praying it wasn't Judith. That somehow she'd found out.

'Nick?' It was a woman, not Judith. I didn't recognize the voice although it was very familiar.

'Yes.'

'It's Jane.'

Jane. Who the fuck was Jane? I didn't know any Janes. It would be just my luck to have a secret admirer choose that moment to tell me she'd been lusting after my pure white body for months. 'Jane?' I said.

'Jane. Jane Hornby. Née Harris. Laura's sister. You do remember Laura, don't you?'

That was a bastard thing to say but I didn't take the bait. If Laura had been a bit of a bitch, Jane was the super-bitch of the family. Apart from their sodding mother, of course, who'd never liked or trusted me and had proved herself gloriously

16

correct, much to her own satisfaction. I think the fact that Mum had caught me drunk one night just before the wedding with my hand up Jane's skirt hadn't helped much. Jane had wanted a fuck that evening, big time, and had never forgiven me either for trying or being caught, I was never sure which.

'Hello, Jane,' I said.

'I take it you've heard.' Just like that. No tears, no nothing. Just 'I take it you've heard.'

'I've heard,' I said. 'I just had a bloke on from Chicago. I'm sorry.'

'Save it,' said Jane. 'If you'd—'

'Don't, Jane,' I interrupted. 'Don't say anything you might regret.'

'I couldn't,' she said. 'I couldn't regret anything I said to or about you. You killed her, Nick, as sure as if you'd shot her. But that's not why I'm calling. Where's Judith? She's staying with you, isn't she?'

'At a friend of mine's, with his wife and kids,' I replied. 'She stays there when she visits me. There's no room here.'

'Does she know?'

'Not from me. I just heard myself. She'll be in bed. Charlie and Ginny run a tight ship.'

'Are you going to tell her? She has to know.'

She was getting on my nerves. 'Of course she has to know. Of course I'll tell her. Who else?'

'I was just checking, Nick. I spoke to the man from the airport too. I've just put the phone down. Laura left my name and number with the airline as well as yours. Obviously she didn't trust you. Someone has to go over there. Make the arrangements to get them home. Louis has no one here. No brothers or sisters. John and I will go.' John was Jane's husband. They had no children. I'm not surprised. I doubted if they'd ever had a fuck together. He was a keen gardener. She was as cold as ice. But then she hadn't always been. I can still remember the way she clamped her thighs so tightly on my hand, that night so long ago, to keep it between her legs.

'I could go,' I said.

'I don't think so, Nick, do you? Mother would have kittens. Besides, you need to look after your daughter. And, talking about her, what do you intend to do?'

'What about?'

'About Judith, of course. She's your responsibility now, and will be until she's at least eighteen.'

Christ, I'd never thought about that, I thought. 'I haven't had time to think,' I said. 'It's all happened so fast.'

'Think about it, Nick. For once you've got to act like an adult. Seagram International are putting us on a plane this morning at ten. We're going straight to Chicago. I'll call you when we get to the hotel. This will take a good few days, I just hope we're back in time for Christmas. I'll speak to you later.' And she hung up.

Yeah, I thought as I switched off the phone my end. We wouldn't want you to miss the turkey, would we?

3

Then I phoned Charlie's house. After a long time a sleepy-sounding woman answered. It was Ginny, Charlie's missus.

'This had better be good,' she said. 'At this time in the morning.'

Like I'd said to Jane, a tight ship, with no messing.

'Ginny,' I said. 'It's Nick. Nick Sharman.'

'I might've guessed. What is it this time? Your car broken down on the North Circ? Can't you just call the AA?'

'It's nothing like that,' I replied. 'Is Charlie there?'

'If he wasn't at twenty to four in the morning, I'd want to know the reason why. Hold on.'

I heard her speaking and a masculine grunt, and Charlie came on. 'Nick. What's up?'

'It's Laura, Charlie,' I replied. 'And Louis and little David. They're dead.' And the truth suddenly hit me and I sobbed and sat down on the bed.

'Nick, I'm half asleep. Say that again.'

So I did, and it didn't get any easier.

'What happened?'

So I told him that too, and he didn't interrupt once.

'I'm sorry, mate,' he said when I stopped. 'So sorry. What about Judith?'

'I need to come over and tell her. But don't wake her. What time do the kids get up?'

'On Saturday, early. There's cartoons on TV. I dunno, seven-thirty, eight.'

'Don't let her see the news.'

'They don't, Nick. Not as a rule. *Power Rangers* is the show of choice.'

'OK. Listen, can I come over soon? I need someone to talk to . . .'

''Course. We won't go back to sleep now. I'll get the kettle on. Come over as soon as you like. I'll make the tea like my old granny did in the Blitz. Lots of rum and sugar.'

'Sounds great,' I said, and put down the phone.

4

I got dressed then, collected my car keys and headed for Charlie's. Although the heater was on full-blast, my heart was as cold as ice. He was watching out of the living-room window as I parked up, and he let me in. He closed the front door quietly and gave me a hug before beckoning me to follow him into the kitchen. Ginny was there sipping at a steaming mug, which she put down when we were inside with the door shut, and she gave me a hug too.

'I'm so sorry, Nick,' she said. 'And that crack when I answered the phone . . .'

'Forget it,' I said. 'I hate those late-night calls too.'

'I should've known something was wrong.'

'You weren't to.' And to avoid any further embarrassment I said, 'So where's this tea then?'

Charlie poured me a mug and laced it heavily with dark rum. But even that couldn't warm the pit of my stomach. I reiterated what I'd told them before and we sat at the kitchen table and waited for the time to pass, drinking more tea and smoking too many cigarettes.

At seven-twenty we heard movement upstairs and Ginny went into the hall. I heard voices, then she came back with Judith.

'Daddy, what are you doing here?' she said in a bewildered voice, and Ginny motioned for Charlie to go outside with her and they left Judith and me alone.

'Darling,' I said. 'I'm so sorry. There's been an accident.' I didn't know how to put it any better.

Judith's eyes widened. 'Mummy . . .' she said.

I nodded. 'And Louis and David too. A plane crash . . .'

I saw Judith start to go, then, and I moved forward and caught her in my arms. How could I have put it any differently? How could I have saved her the shock and the look of pain in her lovely eyes?

'Are they . . . ?' she whispered.

'Yes. I had a call from Chicago. A nice man . . .' What a stupid thing to say.

I steered my daughter to a chair and poured her a cup of tea from the fourth pot that Charlie had made. She ignored it. 'But how?' she said.

'Bad weather. Pilot error. Engine failure. I don't know. Auntie Jane is going over this morning. She'll tell us more when she finds out.'

'I want to go . . .'

'No,' I said. 'It's all been arranged. You stay here.'

'But, Daddy . . .'

'Judith,' I said, sitting opposite her and taking one of her cold hands in both of mine. 'It won't do any good. Let's just wait and let Auntie Jane handle it.'

'But, Daddy . . .' And she started to cry then and I held her tight and felt my tears mingle with hers as they dripped to the floor.

5

Charlie and Ginny left us alone for half an hour, then Ginny knocked on the door and came in.

'Sorry,' she said. 'But I need to make some breakfast . . .'

''Course,' I replied. 'We shouldn't . . .'

'Don't be silly, Nick.' And she opened the fridge and got out the eggs and bacon and butter and all the normal things. 'You want some?'

I looked at Judith, who just shook her head, and Ginny stopped what she was doing and came over and gathered my daughter up in her arms and that started Judith off again, and soon Ginny was weeping too and I didn't know what the hell to do except light yet another cigarette and watch.

In the end I got up and put some bacon under the grill, found the frying pan and started to cook their breakfast myself.

'You don't have to,' said Ginny.

'I know,' I said. 'But it's something to do.' And pretty soon the kitchen was full of the smell of food, which just made me nauseous, and I went out into the back garden and stood in the freezing air and looked at the world gone pear-shaped yet again.

When I went back in, Judith and Ginny were gone and Charlie was serving the food on to plates. 'We've told the kids,' he said. 'They'll leave you alone. Judith's upstairs getting packed.'

'Packed?' I said.

'She's moving back in with you.'

'There's no room.'

22

'You tell her that. She's got a lot of you in her, Nick. Once she decides something . . .'

I went upstairs into the bedroom she was sharing with Sally, Charlie and Ginny's eldest girl, where Judith was neatly folding clothes into her suitcase. 'Sweetheart,' I said. 'Are you sure?'

'Dad, if I can't go with Auntie Jane I'm staying with you. Christ, it's Christmas next week!'

I don't think I'd ever heard her swear like that before. 'It's so small at the flat,' I said weakly.

'Come on,' she said, standing with a sweater in her hands. 'We are related.'

'But you're so grown-up now.'

Truth to tell, probably more grown-up than me.

'Are you embarrassed?' she asked.

I nodded.

'Oh, Daddy!' she said, dropping the jumper and coming over and holding me tight. 'You're so silly.'

She reminded me so much of her mother, then, that my eyes filled again and I put my face into her clean-smelling hair and we stood there in the middle of the room, and it was almost as if she were the parent and I was the child.

6

We drove home in silence. When we stopped outside my flat I told Judith about the TV coverage.

'I want to see it, Dad,' she said.

'It's not very pleasant,' I said. 'But if you feel you have to . . .' What else was there to say? She was growing up. Fast. And all the faster now.

We went upstairs and Judith put on the TV, but it being Saturday morning it was all kid's stuff and she turned down the volume and started to unpack.

Then the phone rang. My first thought was the newspapers, so I answered with a non-committal 'Hello.'

'Mr Sharman,' said a male voice with a cultured accent.

'Who wants him?'

'My name is McAllister. I'm a solicitor.'

'Ambulance-chasing?'

'I beg your pardon?'

'Nothing.'

He seemed genuinely confused. 'Am I by any chance speaking to Mr Nicholas Sharman?' he asked.

'That's me.'

'Good. Mr Sharman, I'd like to meet you. I have a client who would be interested in employing you.'

'I'm not taking any work at the moment.'

Judith gave me a questioning look.

'I see. Even so, I think it would be to our mutual advantage to meet. I might be able to tempt you.'

'I doubt that.'

'I'm sorry. Have I caught you at a bad time?' Understatement of the year. 'I realize it's the weekend and all . . .'

'The day of the week's got nothing to do with it. It's personal.'

'I see . . .'

Judith had come close and she covered the mouthpiece with her hand. 'Daddy,' she said. 'If it's a job, take it. We might need the money.'

'We, white man?' I said. 'It's probably just serving a summons.'

'Find out.'

Fancy being bullied by a fifteen-year-old, I thought, but when she took her hand away I said, 'When?'

'I'm sorry . . . ?'

'The meeting. My business associate has just informed me we *are* taking work after all.'

'I thought you worked alone?'

'This is a relatively new phenomenon.'

'Monday would suit. Ten o'clock at my office.'

'Which is where?'

He gave me an address in Holborn. 'Ten o'clock,' he said.

'Sounds OK, but I might have to change it. Personal reasons.'

'You'll find I'm very flexible, Mr Sharman,' he said. 'Until Monday, then.'

'Until Monday,' I replied, and we broke the connection.

7

Saturday afternoon/Sunday

We caught the lunchtime news, on which the plane crash was the lead story. The news reader said that there had been seven British passengers on board, but no names were mentioned. Judith cried. She cried a lot that weekend and it almost broke my heart. I cried too, and we did our best to comfort each other. But truth to tell, we weren't much help.

Over that Saturday and Sunday we were deluged by phone calls from the media. In the end I just turned on the answerphone and cut the volume. There were some rings on the doorbell too, but I ignored them. I also cancelled Judith's flight to the States. Every so often I checked the answerphone tape and on Sunday afternoon I found a call from Jane in Chicago. She left a phone number and I dialled it back when Judith went to have a shower. It was the Sheraton Hotel and they put me through to her room. She answered on the third ring. 'You just caught us,' she said. 'We have to go to the airline office. It's bedlam here. Newspaper reporters and TV people everywhere. They're having to smuggle us in and out.'

'We've had our share too. Someone put two and two together from the passenger list. We've had some visitors, but I haven't answered the door. And I'm not answering the phone.'

'Keep Judith out of it as much as possible, won't you?'

'Of course. What do you think I'm doing?' I hesitated. 'What about the bodies?'

'We can't see them. They're too badly burned. It looks like identification by other means.'

'Were they definitely on the plane?'

'It looks like it. They checked in . . .'

'But that doesn't always mean . . .'

'Nick. They're dead. My sister is dead. Face it. I've had to.' And I could hear her sob over all those thousands of miles and suddenly it didn't matter that she was a bitch.

'I'm so sorry, Jane,' I said. 'I know you probably think I don't care . . .'

'I'm sorry too, Nick,' she said. 'And I know that you do. Suddenly everything else seems so unimportant.' She sobbed again, then pulled herself together. Back to something more like the old Jane. 'Is Judith there?' she asked.

'She's in the . . . No. Hold on,' I said as Judith came into the room in her dressing gown, towelling her hair. 'She's here now.'

'Auntie Jane,' I said passing the receiver over.

'Hello,' said Judith. 'Auntie Jane. How are you?'

A pause.

'I know. I can't believe it either. What's it like over there?'

A longer pause.

'Have you seen them?'

Short pause.

'But you're sure . . .'

Funny how we all ask the same questions. Where the hell else would they have been?

'Will you ring back later?'

A short pause again.

'OK, Auntie Jane, I'll talk to you then,' and she put the phone down. When she turned round she was crying again. 'Oh, Daddy,' she said. 'Why did this have to happen?'

8

Sunday evening

I got Chinese takeaway for supper that evening, and we sat indoors with the curtains drawn and listened to music on the stereo. It was very quiet inside the house, and I turned the volume down low. 'How are you feeling?' I asked Judith when she pushed away her plate of food that she'd hardly touched.

'Bloody awful. How about you?'

'The same. Listen, Judith. We can nish this meeting tomorrow if you like. With this solicitor geezer.'

'No, Dad. Let's get out of here. I can't stand being cooped up any longer.'

'I don't blame you. OK, we'll go. But I don't fancy taking on any work.'

'Let's see what the offer is.'

All of a sudden she reminded me of Laura. Always the sensible one. Pragmatic. 'Sweetheart,' I said. 'Your mum and me . . .'

She looked at me through Laura's eyes. 'Yes, Dad?'

'I did love her, you know.'

'I know.'

'Never stopped, really. It broke my heart when she slung me out. Divorced me. And it broke my heart again when she remarried. I always hoped . . . maybe one day we'd get back together.'

'I know that too.'

'But it was never her fault. She could be a cow. Well, you know that.'

Judith nodded.

'But it was me. I screwed up that marriage big time.'

'Why?'

'Because I thought I was the greatest. Jack the Lad. Mr Big Time. But I wasn't. I was just a bent copper who dragged a fine woman down with him.'

'But there were other women as well.'

Icy fingers clenched my heart again. 'Oh yeah. Plenty. Plenty of them. I was stupid, Judith. But I thought I'd paid. You see, I believe in the old saying: "What goes round, comes round". Some people call it karma, but that's too hippie bullshit for me. But I really *do* believe that we pay for what we do. Somehow. And I thought I'd paid. Finally. Everyone I've lost. But obviously I haven't. Maybe I never will until I'm dead myself.'

She held my hand tightly. 'Don't say that, Daddy,' she said. 'I couldn't bear to lose you too.'

'No, Judith. Not for a long time. Only the good die young. The really bad people, God keeps them around for as long as possible and takes away everything and everybody they care about. Dying seems to be easy. Carrying on living is the hard thing.'

9

Monday morning

We left the house at about nine on Monday morning for the appointment with McAllister. I was wearing a navy blue suit, pale blue shirt, black tie, black shoes and socks. Judith was wearing a short black skirt, black tights, a black polo-neck sweater and a black leather jacket. But, then, she often did. It was her style. Her hair had been brushed until it shone and she looked gorgeous, although there were faint dark circles under her eyes, which still glistened from time to time.

Jane had phoned again the previous night, late. When Judith was already in bed, asleep. There was not a lot more they could do in Chicago. The bodies would have to stay until formal identification had been made. But, as she told me quietly, from what she could gather, the crash and subsequent fire had been so devastating that it was pick and mix. And the remains that came back could quite easily not be the people they were supposed to be. 'I don't want to fly again after hearing some of the stories,' she said. 'We'll have to this once, but never again for me if I can help it. It scares me, Nick. There's always the chance you'll end up like the people on that plane.'

I didn't pass on any of the news or Jane's sentiments to Judith. Just told her that she was coming home.

We drove up to Holborn and I found a meter near Lincoln's Inn. 'What are you going to do?' I asked Judith.

'Can I come in with you?'

''Course.'

We walked a quarter-mile or so to the street where McAllister had his office and found it with no trouble, it was part of a three-storeyed Georgian house in a leafy side street. 'Must be doing well,' I said as we buzzed for entry.

We were met by a good-looking young blonde and taken straight through to his office at the back of the building, overlooking a small, winter-bare garden.

McAllister was in his thirties, smartly suited in something from Bond Street, complete with waistcoat and gold watch-chain and black shoes.

He stood to greet us and gave Judith a puzzled look. 'My associate,' I explained. 'My daughter, Judith.'

'This is a rather delicate matter, Mr Sharman,' said McAllister when we were all seated and coffee had been ordered.

'One day, everything I have will be hers,' I replied. 'She can stay.'

'If you insist, although it's all rather unorthodox.'

'That's how I run my life.'

'So I've heard.'

He sat back and made a steeple with his fingers.

'I have a client,' he explained. 'An American. Until you have agreed to take the job I'm offering he will remain anonymous. He is over here on a business trip. There have been some threats. He needs . . . How can I put it . . . ?'

'A minder,' I said.

'Exactly. A minder. Your name keeps coming up as the only man in London who could do the job properly.'

'Why's that?'

He looked at Judith. 'My client has some powerful enemies. Violent men. You seem to have the qualifications to deal with such men. From your history, I mean.'

31

'I don't want to get into a fight,' I said. 'I think I'll pass.'

Judith looked at me.

'The remuneration is commensurate with the work,' said McAllister. 'Five thousand pounds per day for the minimum of a week. Ten thousand a day after that.'

'Very nice,' I said. 'Santa's coming just a teeny bit early this year.'

McAllister smiled to show gleaming white teeth. 'Isn't he just.'

'I still think that I must refuse,' I said. 'There has been a tragedy in the family.'

'I'm so sorry,' said McAllister. 'I guessed something as much. But I would ask you to take the time to meet my client. He's staying at the Intercontinental. He is desirous of meeting you there tomorrow for breakfast.'

Desirous. I liked that. Real solicitor-speak.

'I don't think so . . .' I said.

'Daddy?' interrupted Judith. 'It wouldn't hurt to go.'

I gave her a stern look.

'You can always say no then.'

I looked at McAllister and shrugged. 'OK,' I said. 'My associate has given it the thumbs-up.'

'I think you should go alone,' he said. 'My client expressly stated he wants to speak only to you.'

I shrugged again. 'All right,' I said. 'My associate can wait in the coffee shop.'

10

McAllister gave me his client's name then. It was Jefferson Parker of New York City. It meant nothing to me. He had taken a penthouse suite at the Intercontinental. That did. It meant he had money or access to it.

After we left the office, we walked back through the cold morning air to the car and I said, 'Fancy a drink?'

'Coffee?' said Judith.

I looked at my watch. It was almost eleven. 'I fancy something stronger,' I said, feeding more coins into the slot. 'Pubs'll be open in a minute.'

'I thought you might,' she said, and we walked deeper into Holborn and found a boozer where a barman was just opening up, and I got a pint and an orange juice for Judith, and we perched on a couple of seats close to a fake open fire.

'I don't know about all this,' I said.

'Daddy. You need the money. It's a fortune.'

'But not the aggro. It sounds like it might be dangerous. And you need looking after. I haven't got time to take on any work.'

'It's only for a few days.'

'But it's Christmas.'

'We'll survive.'

'Will we? I've got to get you sorted out.'

She lost it then for a moment and tears squeezed out from between her eyelids. 'I love you,' she said.

'And I love you.'

After we'd finished our drinks we went back to the car and headed home. The answerphone tape was full of messages again. But only one seemed worth answering. It was from someone called John Condie. He'd left an Aberdeen phone number and stressed that it was urgent that he spoke to me.

I called him straight back. The telephonist answered with the words 'Condie and Company', and she put me through.

'Mr Sharman,' he said in a strong Scots accent when I'd introduced myself. 'I'm devastated by what's happened. I was a friend of Louis's. Have been since school. We go back a long way. How is Judith?'

'Not bad,' I said. 'Considering.'

'She's a lovely girl. You must be very proud of her.'

'I am.'

'I hate to raise this so soon, but we have business together, Mr Sharman. I'm a solicitor up here in Aberdeen. Louis's solicitor, and Laura's too. I prepared their wills for them and am executor. Of course, we didn't expect a tragedy like this to happen. But they were prepared. Louis left everything to Laura, who in her turn divided her estate between David and Judith. Now, with all the other three in the family gone, everything goes to her on her majority. Until then, I presume you are her legal guardian?'

'Yes.'

'Excellent. We need to meet at some point, Mr Sharman. There's no rush, but we must consider Judith's future. The estate is quite extensive.'

'How extensive?'

'If the family house were to be sold ... I doubt whether Judith could stay there on her own even if she would wish to ... I'd say somewhere in the region of half a million pounds. Louis was a careful man. He made several wise investments. And there's the insurances. Obviously the house mortgage was covered, and there were other policies. Plus, of course,

34

travel insurance. And if the airline is found to be at fault, then the sky's the limit . . . I'm sorry, I didn't mean to be facetious. But American courts can be very generous. *If* it gets to court. The airline may wish to settle quietly.'

'So she won't starve.'

'No, Mr Sharman. Under no circumstances. What about school, by the way?'

'What about it?'

'She's fifteen. Next summer she sits her exams. It's a vital time for her. Will you want her to transfer or stay at school up here?'

'I hadn't thought about it.'

'Well. She's going through a bad time. A change of school could be very disruptive. Of course, she'll be a very rich young woman in a couple of years. But if she's considering university, this coming year is very important.'

'I'll have to talk to her, Mr Condie.'

'John, please. We have to work together now, for the good of your daughter. Let's not be too formal.'

'John,' I said. 'Let me discuss this with her. I'll call you back later in the week.'

'Fine. And please pass my condolences to her. We've become quite good friends since the family moved up here.'

'I'll do that,' I said, and we made our farewells and both hung up.

In the region of half a million quid, I thought as I looked at the phone. And a very nice region to be in. I looked round my flat and wondered what region I was in. Thirty bob to two quid. Maybe I was doing something wrong.

11

Monday afternoon/Tuesday morning

I didn't tell Judith right away about the call I'd made to the solicitor in Scotland. I figured she had enough on her mind to keep her occupied.

That afternoon we got another call from Jane in Chicago. She was at the airport and would get in touch as soon as she arrived home. Judith and I spent the rest of the day inside the flat, ignoring the phone, watching TV and playing long games of cards for matchsticks.

The next morning, early, I got into my suit again and we drove up to Park Lane, where snow lightly dusted the park, and I left the car in the Intercontinental car park. I told the geezer there to charge it to Mr Parker's bill.

I took Judith to the coffee shop, where she settled down with a pot of tea and a couple of magazines, and went upstairs to Jefferson Parker's suite.

It was nine-thirty when I tapped gently on the door and a moment later it was opened by a big black guy in a big black suit, a black shirt, white tie with a Windsor knot and shiny black patent boots. He had 'gangster' written all over him and I almost laughed. 'I'm looking for Mr Parker,' I said. 'Nick Sharman. I'm expected.'

He didn't say a word, just gestured for me to come inside, all cosy like the spider to the fly, and I did just that. He stepped back and I crossed the threshold, brushing past him as I did so to confirm my suspicion that the bulge under his left arm was a weapon. It sure felt like it. Welcome to Rancho

Notorious. As I pushed the door closed behind me, I found myself in the sitting room of the suite. The curtains were closed against the December weather and the view across London, and the room was dimly lit. There were two big settees, two armchairs, a dining table that was littered with papers, and a serving trolley close up to it between two upright chairs. A large-screen TV mumbled to itself in the corner. There were complimentary flowers and fruit every-where, and to the left and right were a pair of doors that I assumed led into the bedrooms. Sweet as a nut and not much change out of a grand a night, I guessed. It was all right for some.

'Is he here?' I asked, after a moment that seemed to stretch like chewing-gum.

The big black geezer nodded and I walked over to one of the settees, pushed a copy of the *International Herald Tribune* on to the floor, sat down and lit a cigarette. 'Got an ashtray?' I said.

He fetched me one and plonked it down on the arm of the sofa. 'Thanks,' I said.

I sat and smoked for a minute and the big black bloke stood and looked at me and never as much as offered me a glass of sparkling mineral water. The whole deal was beginning to get on my tits and I said, 'So where is he?'

'I'm right here, Mr Sharman,' said a voice with a throaty American accent from behind me, and I turned to see a tall black man in a white silk shirt, sans tie and open at the neck, grey suit trousers held up by thin red braces and black, shiny shoes, come through the door in the right-hand wall of the sitting room. 'Sorry to keep you waiting. I had some calls to attend to.' He headed across the carpet with his mitten extended and I stood and shook it. 'Jefferson Parker, New York City,' he said. 'I've heard a lot about you.'

'Which is more than I can say about you,' I said. 'You're a bit of a mystery man.'

'Not at all, Mr Sharman. My life is an open book.' A real charmer. So why didn't I trust him? Maybe it was the big, silent black geezer with what I was sure was a gun under one arm. 'Breakfast, Mr Sharman?' he said. 'It's all keeping warm. Eggs, bacon, hot rolls. You name it.'

'No thanks,' I said. 'I've already eaten.' I had, too. Judith had made me a bacon sandwich and a cup of tea before we'd left.

'I think I'll just have a mouthful,' he said. 'Isaac.'

The big black geezer went to the serving trolley, took off the top and started putting delicate portions of food on to a plate. He was a real Little Lord Fauntleroy underneath it all.

'Coffee, then?' said Parker, like the maître d' from hell.

'Stick it,' I said, stubbing out my cigarette. 'I understand you need some security.' I looked over at the big geezer. 'But it seems to me you have all the security you need.'

'Not at all. Isaac here has to return to New York tomorrow or the next day latest to take care of some business for me.'

Business, I thought. Fucking hell. What kind of business would the dude be taking care of? Not making an after-lunch speech to the Daughters of the American Revolution, that was for sure.

'Listen,' I said. 'I just wanted to make it clear to you that I don't do this sort of thing any more. I've got my own problems to deal with right now, anyway. So why not find someone else? Someone who wants the job.'

'I want you, Mr Sharman.'

'Christ. How many more times? The answer's no. Get me?'

I turned to go, and fucking Isaac decided to get into the act by putting down the plate he was holding and pulling out some fat automatic pistol from just where I guessed he had one and aiming it at my head. 'Listen to Mr Parker,' he said in a voice that sounded like a crowbar being dragged over rusty razor blades, and was more Kingston, Jamaica, than Manhattan Island.

'For fuck's sake,' I said, looking down the barrel of the gun which had to be at least a .45 calibre, judging by the size of the black hole at the end. 'Do me a favour. You're not going to shoot that thing in the suite of a five-star hotel. Not without a silencer at least. So put the fucking thing away and let me get out of here.'

I saw Parker nod, out of the corner of my eye, and Isaac lowered the gun.

Fractionally. That was when I got really pissed off and did what he least expected: I reached over and wrenched the thing out of his hand and hit him between the eyes with the butt. A dangerous thing to do for several reasons. Then, spades having hard heads, I hit him again and he dropped to the floor. Before Parker could move, I reversed the gun and pointed it at him. 'Now me, on the other hand,' I said, 'I don't give a fuck. I'd shoot the fucking thing anywhere. So sit down, Mr Parker, and tell me what's really going on.'

Parker did as he was told, crossed his legs neatly and looked up at me. 'Mind if I smoke?' he asked.

'Go ahead. It's your room.'

He lit up a Marlboro and breathed out smoke in a grey cloud. 'I'm here for a reason, Mr Sharman,' he said. 'Not a reason of my own choosing, but a good reason nevertheless. I have to attend to certain business in this country and I need someone with me who can guide me in the right direction. You are that man.'

'With sodding guns all over the place. I don't think so,' I replied. 'In fact, I think I'll be going now.' And I ejected the magazine from the gun and dropped it into the coffee pot, cleared the bullet that was in the chamber and tossed the gun itself into the corner of the room. 'See you later,' I said as I opened the door to the hall, only to be confronted by two men in dark suits who were flanking Judith. One was tall and fat, the other was short and thin.

They both took warrant cards out of their pockets and flashed them at me. The tall guy's one was regular Met. The other's contained a gold badge. The taller of the two said in a cockney accent, 'Stay where you are, Mr Sharman. We're the law.'

12

'If this is a bust, I'm innocent,' I said. 'I just got here. Ask her.'

'This isn't a bust,' said the taller one and came into the room, pushing Judith gently in front of him. He shut the door and introduced himself: 'Detective Superintendent Latimer from West End Central. This is Harry Shapiro, Lieutenant Harry Shapiro, NYPD.'

'Cool,' I said. 'This is just like TV. Is Jimmy Smits outside getting his make-up on?'

Shapiro laughed through his nose. 'A wise guy,' he said. 'Just what I fuckin' need.'

'Not in front of my daughter,' I said. 'You're not in New York City now.'

Shapiro wrinkled his brow then turned to Judith. 'Sorry, miss,' he said. 'I'm out of practice in dealing with young ladies.'

Judith took it totally in her stride. She was growing up before my very eyes. 'That's OK, Mr Shapiro. Daddy says that all the time.'

'Can we cut the happy-family stuff?' said Latimer. 'Let's get this over and done with. Everybody sit down.'

I did as I was told, perching on the arm of the settee opposite Parker as Judith sat demurely next to me.

Latimer went to the coffee pot and Shapiro stood over Isaac, who was moaning gently.

'You do this?' he said to me.

I nodded.

'You must be good,' said Shapiro. 'But don't get downwind of him in a hurry. He's killed for less than a smack on the noggin.' His accent was becoming more New York Irish as he spoke.

'Shapiro?' I said. 'That's not Irish.'

He got my drift. 'Mother married a guy from the garment district. He was Jewish. She insisted we were brought up as Catholics. It got confusing round Christmas time.'

I was beginning to like the geezer.

Latimer was getting more impatient. As he swung the coffee pot about, he heard metal grating inside. 'What the hell's that?' he said, peering inside with a frown.

'The clip from Sleeping Beauty's gun,' I said. 'But it shouldn't spoil the taste.'

He banged the coffee pot down in disgust and sat next to Parker.

'So what's the deal?' I asked.

41

Parker looked at the two police officers and then at me. 'I'm a broker in high-risk, high-profit consumer durables,' he explained.

I had to laugh and he almost looked hurt. 'Is that right?' I said. 'Let me think ... From all this,' I gestured round the room, 'and the goon on the floor, and the two coppers from different time zones, I'm going to guess it's not teddy bears for Bosnian babies.'

'Not exactly,' said Parker.

'Cut the crap, Parker,' said Shapiro. 'You ain't runnin' this show, just remember that.' Then to me, 'Our friend here is a big-time drug dealer in the Apple. And I mean *big* time. He's involved with all his homeboys from JA. Yardies, you call them. But they're just the same old scumbags to me.' At that moment, Isaac began to come to with a groan, and Shapiro helped him to his feet and pushed him down on the other side of Parker. 'Sit still and shut up, stupid,' the New York copper said, and Isaac did as he was told, but the looks he gave me could've stripped paint. 'Mr Parker made a big mistake a few months ago,' Shapiro went on, 'that left half a dozen guys dead on a little farm in New Jersey. And his buddies put out a contract on him. A most lucrative contract that had every low-life in the city checking that his gun was loaded. Naturally he came running to us. To me. Scum like him always do.' Parker looked offended, but Shapiro ignored him. 'I'm in control of a small department linked to the DEA. Very small, very exclusive. We're not interested in some junkie dealing a little to support his own habit. We go for big-timers. Like Mr Parker. He wanted to exchange what information he had for a new life somewhere quiet. Very commendable. But I had other ideas. I was over here earlier this year helping out my good friends at the Metropolitan Police. They've been having

42

trouble with Yardies too. Glocks and Sigs on the streets of old London town. And loads of drugs. It was getting just like back home. Anyway, Mr Parker told us that he had big dealings with one or two players here, so I figured that maybe we could be of some use. Naturally he jumped at the idea . . .'

By the look on Parker's face, I somehow doubted that.

'. . . So I got in touch with Superintendent Latimer and here we are.'

'And me?' I asked.

'You helped clear up a case some time ago for the Met,' said Latimer. 'You know the territory. We thought you might like to help us again.'

'I was coerced into getting involved in the case by a bunch of renegade coppers who weren't quite sure which side of the law they were on. It ended up with about twenty people dead, and me almost being put away for a long stretch of porridge. And now you want me to sign on again. I don't think so.'

'We just assumed that as a concerned citizen—'

'You assumed wrong,' I interrupted. 'Come on, Judith, we're going home.'

13

'Not so fast,' said Latimer. 'Let me put my cards on the table—'

'No. Let me,' interrupted Parker.

I looked at him.

'Mr Sharman,' he said. 'Before I came here I made some enquiries. I have friends over here. And legal advisers.'

'McAllister,' I said.

'Precisely. As I told you, all this was not my idea. But I was ... am ... between a rock and a hard place. My life is in danger. I have agreed to help the *federales*. But I need someone who is familiar with what goes on over here at street level. Without that someone, I would rather take my chances alone.'

'What about Isaac?' I said.

Shapiro sniggered. 'Sergeant Isaac Lopez, also of the NYPD. Did you think your people would let anyone tote a gun round this burg without official permission? Not that it did him much good.' He sniggered again. 'Isaac here works undercover. We put him in with Parker two months ago, when all this first blew up.'

'He's not much good is he?' I said.

'Not the greatest. But he has little regard for you Limeys. Maybe a bit more now, huh, Isaac?'

Isaac just sneered in my direction.

'And besides,' Shapiro continued, 'he has to get back to sort out some details. And a doctor's appointment, hey, Izzy?'

'The offer of the money still stands,' said Parker. 'That is my *personal* money.'

'Not if the IRS gets there first,' said Shapiro. He seemed to be enjoying the whole set-up, as was proved when he took the lid off the serving trolley and made himself a bacon roll. 'You want something, honey?' he said to Judith. 'Coke or something?'

'Please,' said Judith. She still has an insatiable thirst for sweet drinks.

'There should be something in the minibar. Isaac, get the young lady a drink, and whilst you're at it fish your magazine out of the coffee pot. You never know when you might need it.'

'This is getting us nowhere,' I said. 'I'm not interested. Not for money, for glory, nor for the chance to do the right thing.'

Latimer sucked air through clenched teeth. 'All right, Mr Sharman,' he said. 'You're the boss. What you say goes, but it would be easier if you were in.'

'Easier for whom?' I said. 'You. I don't care, mate. All I care about now is my daughter. So when she's finished her drink we'll be off, and frankly if I never see any of you again, it'll be too soon.'

But my old dad always said you should never say never.

14

Wednesday

The next day I took Judith out to do some Christmas shopping. We ate lunch in Selfridges' restaurant. By then she was loaded down with bags from Bond Street and Oxford Street and my credit card had almost expired from overwork.

As she dug into a vegetarian lasagne I thought that it was time to talk about the future. I told her about the call from John Condie in Aberdeen and she looked at me closely as she carefully wiped her mouth. 'I want to live with you, Daddy,' she said.

'At the flat? I don't think so.'

'We'll get a new place. I'll have enough money to buy

somewhere nice if what you say is right.' It was amazing how sensible she was becoming.

'And I live off my daughter? No, Judith. Maybe if I was eighty and dribbled a lot.'

'You do dribble a lot.'

'No I don't.'

'But you could.'

'And school. You've got exams soon.'

'Next summer.'

'It'll be here quicker than you think.'

'I could get a transfer to somewhere in London. There's some great schools down here.'

'You'll lose continuity. Teachers. Friends.'

'I can't go back to the house.'

'No one was suggesting you would. Don't be daft! How about a friend's? Somewhere you could stay for a while.'

She wrinkled her nose. 'No thanks. I'd rather live in cardboard city.'

'It won't come to that.'

'Come up to Scotland.'

'My life's down here.'

'What life?'

It was below the belt, but true. 'Sorry,' she said quickly. 'I didn't mean it.'

'This is crazy,' I said. 'I've got a rich daughter all of a sudden, and we're arguing.'

She started to cry again. I knew then I should've waited to talk, but the warm, crowded atmosphere seemed to me the best place. A middle-aged matron at the next table scowled at me over her steak pie. I shrugged, but I felt like I'd been caught beating Judith up.

'Are you all right?' I asked.

She nodded but the tears continued to plop on to her plate of forgotten food.

'Really?' I said.

'Really. But it's you I'm worried about, Dad. I've seen you like this before. Just drifting around. You need to work. Otherwise you'll brood, and get drunk all the time.'

Charming, I thought. Character assassination now. But of course she was right. 'Something will turn up,' I said, like Mr Micawber. 'Something always does.'

'Something has,' she said. 'And you've turned it down.'

'We'll sort it out, Judith,' I said. 'Don't worry. I won't let you down.'

And I meant it.

When we got back to the house there was a car blocking the entrance to what the tenants euphemistically call the drive, which in fact is an area of hard parking that used to be the front garden. There were two men sitting in the car. When I tooted them they got out. It was Latimer and Shapiro.

'Jesus,' I said to Judith. 'What the hell do they want?' I rolled down my window. 'Can you move your car?' I asked politely. 'I want to get in.'

'Certainly,' said Latimer, and he did so. When I was parked up, they came over to the car.

'Afternoon,' said Latimer. 'We need to talk ... alone.'

'You're wasting your time,' I said.

'Pubs are open,' said Latimer. 'We'll buy you a drink.'

I looked at Judith. 'I'll be fine,' she said. 'I'll go upstairs and try on some of my new clothes.'

'OK,' I said to the two policemen as Judith and I got out of the car and I locked it. 'But I'm not going to change my mind.'

'It's Christmas,' said Shapiro. 'Goodwill to all men.' He

looked at Judith's shopping bags. 'Or young women, by the looks of it.'

Judith grinned. 'I took him for every penny,' she said. 'He's a softie.'

'That's not what I heard,' said Shapiro.

After Judith had gone indoors we all got into Latimer's motor and headed down to Tulse Hill. He parked the car at the back of the Tulse Hill Hotel and we went into the saloon bar, which was about half full, with Johnny Mathis singing 'When A Child Is Born' on the jukebox. Latimer set up the drinks whilst Shapiro and I found an empty table right at the back, as far away from the speakers as was possible. Latimer joined us and passed round his cigarettes.

'What's all this about?' I asked when my cigarette was lit and I'd had the first sip of my pint.

Latimer took a sheaf of papers out of the inside pocket of his overcoat and passed them to me.

'What is it?' I asked, without looking.

'The passenger manifest for Seagram International flight number 713 from New York to Chicago last Friday after-noon.'

I felt a cold hand inside me again, wrenching my guts. 'Is this a joke? Because if it is, I don't appreciate it.'

'It's no joke,' said Latimer. 'Take a look.'

I opened the papers. The first and longest list was the economy class.

'Look in business,' he said.

I did as I was told and found the second list. It was much shorter. Halfway down I read: Louis Rudnick, Laura Rudnick, David Rudnick (infant).

'Yeah,' I said, and my voice sounded strange.

'Now first-class.'

An even shorter list. The last two names were: Jefferson Parker, Isaac Lopez.

'I don't believe it,' I said. 'This is a set-up.'

Shapiro pulled a newspaper from his pocket. It was open to an inside page and folded tight.

'This is from the *New York Times* last Sunday. Two days before we met you.'

It was a list of the passengers on the plane again. The same names appeared as on the list that Latimer had given me.

'Fuck,' I said.

'It took us a while to work it out,' said Latimer. 'The different surnames. I'm very sorry for your loss. And your daughter's. She seems like a good kid.'

'We've been in touch with the FBI,' said Shapiro. 'There was a bomb on the plane. It blew the tail off just as it was coming in to land. Why it was left so late, no one knows. Maybe it was a faulty timer, maybe they wanted it to happen right then at O'Hare. But another thirty minutes and the plane would've been all but empty. By the way, the bomb thing. That's classified. Only a few people know.'

I tapped the paper. 'So where were Parker and Lopez?'

'En route to London under fake ID,' said Shapiro. 'A couple of good men took their place on the Chicago flight. Friends of mine.'

'And you're sure whoever it was was after these two?'

'From the initial FBI findings there was no one else on board who was a likely target. We're going ahead with the assumption that it was our boys they were after.' Shapiro again.

'And they killed my ex-wife, Judith's mother. And her family.'

'Plus nearly four hundred others,' said Latimer. 'But yes.'

'And a couple of days after, the supposed target tries to hire me to work for him.'

Latimer shrugged. 'It's one of those one in a million coincidences that you wouldn't believe in a film.'

'And you think that there's people over here involved?'

'Over here, in the US, and in the islands,' said Latimer. 'They're as thick as thieves, the lot of them.'

'And you still want my help?'

'Sure,' said Shapiro. 'That's why we're here.'

'And the money's still on offer?'

Latimer smiled cynically. 'Still on the table.'

'Well stick it,' I said. 'I'll do this for nothing. Count me in.'

15

'Good,' said Latimer. 'And once again, I'm very sorry.'

'Not as sorry as Judith and me,' I replied. 'What now?'

'Come to the hotel tomorrow morning at the same time and we'll brief you,' said Shapiro.

'I'll be there. I think maybe I'd better go and see Judith now.'

'Are you going to tell her?' asked Latimer.

'I thought the information was classified,' I said sourly. 'Yes, I'm going to tell her. I think she deserves the truth. And I need to make sure she's looked after. It's Christmas at the beginning of next week. Not the happiest Christmas either of us is ever going to have.'

'At least she wasn't on the plane,' said Shapiro.

'There is that,' I said. 'We do have to look on the bright side, don't we?'

I got up then and left the bar. I walked home the long way round, the cold wind whipping at the skirts of my coat as the early dusk fell and the street lights popped on one by one. I stood outside the house and lit a cigarette and looked up at the lighted window of the room where Judith was waiting, and wondered how the hell I was going to break the news to her.

I flipped the cigarette away after just a few drags and went inside.

Judith was watching TV in one of her new outfits. 'Looking good,' I said when she got up and gave me a twirl as I went in. 'Quite the sophisticate.'

'What did they want?' she asked.

'They had something to tell me about the crash.'

'What?'

So I told her. She sat down as I did so and began to cry again.

'I took the job,' I said, when I'd finished. I didn't tell her I was doing it for free. That didn't seem to be necessary.

'Good,' she said. 'I'm glad.'

'But what about you?' I asked.

'What about me?'

'It's going to be dangerous. I don't want you caught up in the crossfire.'

'I'll be all right.'

'These people are bad,' I said. 'Very bad.'

And as I said the words, it occurred to me that Latimer and Shapiro might be lying. Christ, I'd been mugged off enough times before, and I wondered if the passenger manifest they'd showed me had really been legit. I'd just taken their word for it, but like so much else these days, newspaper clippings could be faked. 'I've got to make a call,' I said, and picked up the phone.

I punched in the number of my old pal Chas, who still works for one of the nationals up at Wapping. I got the switchboard and they put me through to his extension. A woman answered and it sounded like there was a riot going on in the background. I asked for Chas and the handset went down with a clunk and I held on for what seemed like ages. Eventually he came on the line. 'What's going on?' I asked when he spoke. 'World War Three?'

'Office party,' he replied. 'What's up, Nick?'

'You heard what happened to Laura?'

'Hold on.'

The phone went down again and the background sound diminished as I imagined he closed the door of his office on the revelries. 'That's better,' he said when he returned. 'Journalists ... Bloody lunatics ... Of course I heard ... I'm truly sorry, Nick ... I tried to call but got no answer.'

'For a story?' I asked.

'No. As a friend. It's Chas. Remember me?'

'I'm sorry,' I said. 'Bad time.'

'Sure. So what can I do for you?'

'A favour.'

'What?' He sounded suspicious. He'd done favours for me before and regretted them.

'Not much. I need to know about a couple of other passengers on the plane.'

'Something up?'

He always had a nose for a scoop, did Chas.

'Maybe,' I replied. 'Can you get hold of a copy of the passenger manifest?'

'Probably.'

'Now?'

'Hold on. It might still be on the computer. It won't take a sec.' There was a pause. 'Yeah, it hasn't been wiped.'

'And this is gen?'

'Of course. Why do you ask?'

'Maybe nothing. Check first-class.'

'Yeah.'

'Parker and Lopez. They listed?'

'That's right.'

'Thanks, Chas.'

'And that's it, you're just going to leave me hanging? What's going on?'

'Maybe something, maybe nothing, but I promise you'll be the first to know.'

'You always say that.'

'And I always tell the truth. Merry Christmas. Enjoy the party.' And I hung up.

'At least they weren't lying about that,' I said to Judith.

Then the phone rang and I answered it. I expected it to be Chas calling back, but it was Jane.

'We're home,' she said. 'Sorry I haven't called before, but what with the jet-lag and everything else . . .'

'How was it?' I asked inanely.

'How do you think? Frustrating to say the least. We were blocked at every turn, although the authorities were most charming. We'll have to go back. We won't be able to have the funeral till the new year.'

Christ, the funeral. I hadn't even thought about that little future horror.

'We'd like to see Judith,' she went on. 'What are your plans for Christmas?'

'None at the moment. I've just taken on some work . . .'

'Oh good. Another sleazy little case, I suppose?'

I didn't tell her what Shapiro and Latimer had said. 'It's important,' was all I said.

'It would be. Is Judith there?'

'Yes.'

I passed the phone on. 'Jane,' I said, covering the mouthpiece. 'Not a word about what I said.'

'Hello, Auntie Jane,' said Judith when she had the phone. 'Yes, fine. Well, you know . . . How are you?'

'Good. Christmas? With Daddy, but he's got something to do . . . At yours?' she looked at me. 'Well, for a couple of days maybe. I'll talk to Daddy and call you back. You're at home . . . Yes, OK. Bye.' And she put down the phone. 'They want me to visit. Stay for Christmas.' Jane and her husband lived just south of London in an ancient and modern town on the way to Brighton.

'Good idea,' I said. 'What with everything else.'

'You want me to go?'

'No. But at least you'll be safe.'

'Only if you come for Christmas lunch.'

'Where the atmosphere will be as frozen as the turkey.'

'Not from me.'

'I know. OK, darling. If that's the way you want it.'

'I do.'

'Then phone them back. Tell them to pick you up tomorrow. Then I can take care of business.'

16

Wednesday afternoon/Thursday morning

Judith did as I told her, and Jane made an arrangement to pick her up the next day at around eleven. When she put the phone down I switched it off. I didn't want Chas phoning back and asking awkward questions.

'Remember. Not a word about what I said before. There's no point in upsetting Auntie Jane any more than she already is,' I told Judith as she packed a bag of clothes.

'OK, Dad,' she said.

I was getting prouder of her by the day. She was turning into a fine young woman, although how the responsibility she was taking on to her young shoulders would affect her eventually, I had no way of knowing.

The next morning I left her with a kiss and a hug and a promise to call her at Jane's later, and I caught a minicab up to town.

The driver dropped me outside the Intercontinental and I went up to Parker's suite. This time the door was opened by Shapiro, coffee cup in hand. 'Good morning,' he said. 'Everything OK?'

'Not bad. Judith's going down to her aunt's to stay for the holiday.'

'Good idea,' he said as he poured me a cup and I lit a cigarette. 'The others will be joining us in a few minutes.'

There were a couple of bags packed by the door. Shapiro saw me looking. 'Izzy's,' he said. 'He's going back Stateside. Catching a plane in a couple of hours. He'll be back in a few days. We're getting some good intelligence out of Parker. Izzy has to go back and fill in our colleagues on the details. There'll be some major busts at the weekend. Just as the scumbags are sitting round the Christmas tree opening their presents with their loved ones.' His voice was thick with scorn as he spoke. 'I hope some of 'em are carrying. It'll save the cost of a trial.' I decided then and there to try and keep on Shapiro's good side.

'So I'm looking after your boy?'

'That's the plan. Latimer and I have other fish to fry on this side. Big ones. Parker's spilling the beans on some of his British compatriots even as we speak.'

'Good job.'

I smoked my cigarette, and Shapiro and I drank our coffee in silence until the door to one of the other rooms opened and Parker, Lopez and Latimer came in. Latimer was wearing a leather jacket and jeans, Lopez had exchanged his black gangster suit for grey slacks and a sports coat that must've been about a size sixty chest. He had a big plaster on his forehead where I'd hit him and didn't look too happy to see me. Parker was elegant in a blue double-breasted with black loafers.

'Good morning,' said Latimer. 'I've filled these two in on developments.'

'Good,' I said.

Lopez looked at his watch. 'Better be movin' soon,' he growled.

'How are you getting to the airport?' asked Latimer.

'Cab, I guess.'

'Sharman will drive you,' said Latimer.

'Do what?' I said. 'Who am I? The boy?' I didn't relish being a chauffeur for the black detective. For anyone, for that matter. Especially as I was doing this one gratis. And I hated being called Sharman, except by people I looked upon as friends.

'Sorry,' said Latimer. 'I'm used to giving orders.'

'But I'm not used to taking them. Besides, I've got no car,' I said.

'Take ours,' said Latimer. 'It's in the garage downstairs, lower level. We're not going anywhere.'

'I thought we were supposed to be having a meeting,' I protested.

'That can wait,' said Latimer. 'We've got some business to discuss with Mr Parker first. You'll be back in a couple of hours. Lopez is travelling under his own passport this time. American Airlines, full VIP cop treatment. First-class. No customs either end and all the filet he can eat. We can have some lunch when you get back and talk then.'

'Cosy,' I said.

I looked at Lopez. He looked about as happy about being in close proximity to me for an hour as I felt.

'Take him,' said Shapiro. 'Please. Parker will be all right with us.'

'OK,' I said. 'Give me the keys.'

Latimer tossed them over. 'Blue SAAB,' he said.

'I remember,' I said, got up, picked up a tweed overcoat and one of Lopez's suitcases as he got the other, and left the suite. As we walked to the lift I said, 'Listen. About the other day. I didn't know who you were, right?'

'Sure.'

He obviously didn't want to talk about it, so when we got into the lift, I kept quiet as it headed down towards the basement car park.

17

When the lift arrived in the deserted basement garage, we walked across the rubber- and oil-stained floor, looking for Latimer's car. Finally I spotted it in one corner and said, 'There it is, the blue saloon.'

Lopez just grunted in reply. I wasn't looking forward to sitting in any traffic jams with him. What the fuck am I doing here? I thought.

I got out the keys and walked round to the boot, when I heard a faint sound from the shadows, close to the gap where a dim sign proclaimed 'EXIT' in blue neon letters, and the back window of the SAAB imploded: another bullet screeched off the bodywork close to where I was standing, and Lopez, with an amazed look on his face, dropped the bag and coat he was carrying and fell to the ground with a thud. I saw muzzle flashes come from the darkness, but heard only the discreet coughs of silenced gun barrels.

I just stood there for a stunned second before reacting. Then I dropped the bag I was carrying too, ducked down behind the car and peered over the top of the boot.

Lopez was lying a yard or so away from me, scrabbling at the concrete with hands and feet. 'Help me!' he cried gutturally. 'For Christ's sake, help me!'

I had no choice. Risking more bullets, I crabbed away from the car on my hands and knees until I was next to him. I grabbed him by the collar of his jacket and his belt and dragged him awkwardly into the shelter of one of the buttresses that stuck out into the body of the car park. 'Oh shit!' he cried. 'Oh shit, oh fuck, oh Jesus Christ it hurts!'

It looked like it did too. The bullet had hit him dead in the centre of his back and exited through the front of his coat. There was blood spurting from both the entry and exit wounds. I tore off my jacket, ripped off my shirt and made a pad for his chest where most of the blood seemed to be coming from. 'Give me your hand,' I said.

He held up his hand and I placed it over the hole where the bullet had exited him and I pushed his palm hard against the flow of blood. 'Hold that tight,' I said.

'Oh Jesus!' he cried. 'Sweet Jesus help me!'

'Gun!' I screamed. 'Where's your fucking gun?'

'Jesus, please . . .'

'The fucking gun!' I yelled, running my hands under his arm where he'd concealed it before, but felt nothing. Where the fuck did he keep the sodding thing? Or had he left it behind with Shapiro before getting ready for the flight? 'Lopez,' I almost screamed in a whisper. 'Are you armed?'

He stopped calling for divine intervention for a second and pointed with his free hand to his waist. I ran my hands round his belt and felt a concealed holster inside his trousers at the small of his back. I yanked up his jacket and pulled out his .45 automatic. The pistol was huge and heavy, warm from his body heat, and fitted into my hand like it had been custom-made for me. I chambered a round and held the gun in front of me. I heard a sound like a shoe scraping on concrete from behind a parked car and fired, spraying bullets every which way. I heard them clanging on to metal and smashing glass and hoped I didn't hit a fuel tank, or else detective kebab would be on the menu. I also hoped that it wasn't some innocent passer-by investigating the sound of the ambusher's bullets or I might be guilty of sending some civilian to an

59

early grave. Before the clip was empty, I eased my finger off the trigger. I didn't have any spare magazines.

'Mother!' Lopez cried. 'Where are you?'

'She's not here,' I said. 'Shut up.'

'I can see her. Mother!' And he reached out the hand that wasn't pressed to his chest.

'No,' I said.

Then he turned and looked at me. 'Hold me,' he said. 'Hold me, Mother.'

Shit! I thought. He thinks I'm his fucking mum now. Under other circumstances it would've been hysterical. But here, now, it was as sad as shit.

I wiped a bloodstained hand across my face and went closer. I sat with my back against the brick and heaved him to me. He lay across my legs with his back against my chest, and the only thing I could think was that if the gunnie came round the corner, the first bullets would probably finish Lopez off. I held the gun straight out over his shoulder and waited.

'Oh Jesus fuck! Oh fuck, oh fuck, oh God, stop it hurting. Mother, help me!' He wouldn't stop.

I looked down at him and knew he was going fast. 'Momma. Momma. I said we'd be together some day.' He looked up. 'Momma,' he said. 'You look so beautiful.'

I touched his head. 'Don't worry,' I said. 'It'll be all right soon.' There was nothing I could do to help.

'Kiss me, Momma,' he said. 'Give me a kiss.'

I felt like someone was playing a cruel trick on us both.

'Kiss me,' he pleaded.

So I did. I leaned my head forward and gently touched his forehead with my lips. And as I did it, I felt the life ebb out of him and he slumped in my arms.

18

After that I could hear nothing but the ringing in my ears from the gunshots I'd fired.

I sat still for a few minutes with Lopez's dead weight on my legs. Then I pushed him off as gently as I could and slowly stood up. The garage seemed as deserted as when we'd entered it, but I knew how deceptive that could be. I held the gun up in front of me and slowly turned in a half-circle. Still nothing. I picked up my jacket and slipped it on over my blood-soaked clothes. Then, leaving Lopez, who was beyond help, I ran back towards the lift and pressed the button. I stood away from the doors and pointed the gun towards them. Christ knew who might be behind them when they opened.

But the lift was empty. I pressed the button for Parker's floor and stood with my back pressed against the rear wall of the metal box, the gun concealed behind me as it sped upwards.

When the doors opened again the hallway was empty, but for a maid's cart, and I ran down to the suite door.

It was ajar. Was the sodding maid inside or what? Hating every second, I pushed the door open wide.

The sitting room of the suite was a carnage. There was blood everywhere, splattered up the walls and soaking into the carpets and furniture. Someone had got there before me and it certainly wasn't the maid, unless she was fed up with poor gratuities.

Shapiro was lying on the couch face upwards, eyes open and already turning milky-white, the front of his shirt dark with gore. Latimer was on the floor on his front, as still as

Shapiro, and Lopez in the garage. There was no sign of Parker. The whole place stank of used gunpowder and shit and blood.

I closed the door to the corridor and slipped the lock, then tried both doors to the bedrooms. Lopez's was neat and tidy. Parker's showed signs of habitation, but both were empty.

I checked the two dead bodies. Both men had been carrying and both weapons were snug in their holsters. Shapiro's was a Detonics .45. Latimer's a small .38 Colt revolver. I helped myself to both.

Latimer had a mobile phone in one pocket of his jacket. I looked at my watch. It was getting late. My, but how time flies when you're having fun. I punched in my home number. The answerphone was on. I found my address book and tried Jane's number. There was an answerphone there too. Finally, I tried her car phone. She answered on the third ring.

'Hello,' she said.

'Jane. Nick. Where are you?'

'In the car.'

'I know that. But where?'

'On the A23 coming into Croydon. Why?'

'Don't be alarmed, but can you get off the main road and take some side streets until you're sure you're not being followed?'

'*What?*'

'Do it, Jane, please. And let me speak to Judith.'

She came on the line. 'There's been some trouble,' I said. 'I've told Jane to get on to the side roads. You might be being followed. Don't let her go home until you're sure you're not. I know she thinks I'm mad, but believe me, it's important. You'd better tell her about the bomb in the plane. Maybe

62

she'll believe you. And, anyway, it'll be all over the papers soon.'

She was cool. 'Yes, Dad,' was all she said.

'I'm not going to be about for a bit. Look at the news and you'll see why. But don't worry, I'm OK. I didn't have anything to do with what happened, except I was there. No matter what anyone says, I'm telling the truth.'

'I know.'

'Either I'm being set up or I've been very lucky. Just trust me, sweetheart, I'll be in touch as soon as I can. Love you.'

'Love you too,' she replied, and I cut off the phone.

I looked down at my bloodstained clothes and went back into Parker's room. He was about the same size as me and I found a shirt that fitted and changed it for my torn and stained one. I checked his wardrobe and found an overcoat. It was camel-coloured and made of some silky cashmere. It fitted me perfectly, although the three guns and phone I was carrying sagged the pockets slightly, but what could I do?

I checked his bedroom more thoroughly then. In a drawer in a roll-top bureau opposite the bed I found an envelope containing five grand in fifties. Obviously my first day's pay, and equally obviously robbery wasn't the motive for what had gone down.

I pocketed the money, went back into the sitting room, cracked the door to make sure the coast was clear and left.

19

When I got down to the foyer I expected it to be crawling with Old Bill, but all seemed to be normal. I couldn't believe that no one had heard the shots I'd fired in the car park, or found Lopez's body, but obviously they hadn't.

I walked through the main doors, down to Piccadilly and hailed a cab.

'Where to?' said the driver.

Fuck knows, I thought, then had an idea. 'Brixton,' I said. I needed a motor badly, but I needed something else first, and I knew just where to find it.

I sat in the back of the taxi and looked at the 'Thank You for Not Smoking' sign and wanted a Silk Cut desperately, but not a punch-up with the driver, so I fought back the urge and looked out of the window instead as we cruised past Buckingham Palace, through Victoria and over Vauxhall Bridge. And I watched London change from elegant to broken-down, all within ten minutes.

There were Christmas lights in Brixton which did little to cheer the place up and as we passed the market, the driver leaned back and said, 'Whereabouts?'

'Go up Brixton Hill,' I replied. 'I'll tell you where.'

I got him to stop by a big council estate. There was twelve quid on the clock. I took out a twenty, gave it to him and said, 'Leave the clock running and wait for me a minute, will you? I won't be long.'

'What, here?' he said suspiciously.

'That's right. If it gets up to sixteen quid you can go.'

'Fair enough,' he said and pulled out his paper. I got out and cut through a walkway and on to the estate.

The block I wanted was just a minute away and I crossed to the entrance over muddy grass that was crusted with grey snow and frozen dog shit. I climbed one flight of concrete stairs, trotted down the open walkway and knocked on the door of number ten.

There was a light on in the hall but no one answered, so I knocked again. After a minute the door opened on a chain and a tousled head peered through the gap. 'Oh, it's you,' the owner of the head said and pushed the door to, let off the chain, and opened it wide. 'Come on then,' he said. 'It's fucking freezing out there.'

I sidled into the hall, which was warm and smelled of last night's dope. The flat's tenant stood in front of me, resplendent in a pair of baby-blue pyjamas covered with pink teddy bears. Hardly his usual style, which tended more towards leather strides and tattoos. 'Nice jammies,' I commented.

'The bird give 'em to me,' he said, scratching his head.

'She here?'

'I wouldn't be wearing these if she was,' he replied testily. 'What do you want? As if I didn't know.'

'You sorted?' I asked.

''Course.'

'Coke?'

'Sure. How much?'

'Couple of grams. Good gear, mind.'

'No problem. Come on in.'

I followed him into the living room, which looked like it had been ransacked by robbers but was just in its usual state. 'Wait,' he said, and went out into the hall again. He was back in less than a minute with two white wraps in his hand. 'The best in town,' he said. 'Looks like you'll be having a white Christmas.'

'How much?' I asked.

'As it's you and the time of year, one-twenty.'

I took out my wallet and found the cash. 'Cheers,' he said, folding the wedge into the breast pocket of his pyjama jacket. 'Cuppa tea?'

'No thanks, I've got a cab waiting. I'll just have a line. Want some?'

'Too early for me, but go ahead,' he said. And I did, clearing a space on the glass coffee table, cutting out two big lines with a scalpel that was lying on it and snorting them both, using a new tenner.

'You look like you needed that,' he remarked.

'I did. And I'll need it more where I'm going. Listen, I'll see you soon.'

'Sure. Any time. But make it a bit later in the day, will you?'

'I'll try,' I said, and he showed me to the door.

20

When I got back to the cab, the driver was starting the motor to leave. 'Just in time,' he said as I jumped in the back.

'Norwood now, mate,' I said. 'And that'll be me.'

I got him to drop me off round the corner from Charlie's used-car emporium, and walked the rest of the way. Charlie was standing by a second-hand Mercedes estate, wrapped up warm in his sheepskin, drinking from a steaming cup and looking up and down the street as if he could summon customers by sheer force of will.

'Nick,' he said when he saw me. 'I've been trying to ring you, but all I get is the answering machine.'

'I got your messages,' I said. 'Sorry I haven't called back.'

'So how is everything? Judith?'

'She's at her auntie's. Things ain't good.' I told him part of the story, but didn't include the dead bodies back at the hotel. I didn't think he was ready for that. He could catch it on the news later.

'No wonder you look a bit rough,' he said. 'Laura murdered. Christ, that's heavy. Here, have some of this.'

He put his cup down on the Merc's bonnet, hauled a flask out of the back pocket of his trousers and opened it. 'Brandy,' he said.

I took a long swig and felt the liquor burn down into my gut. 'That's good,' I said.

'I like it,' said Charlie, taking the flask back and adding some brandy to his tea. 'So what can I do for you?'

'I need a motor,' I said.

'I was afraid of that. Remember what happened to the last one I lent you? I had a hell of a job convincing Old Bill it was nicked off the front. And what's wrong with yours?'

'I don't think so, Charlie,' I said. 'I'm a bit warm at the moment and I need something cool.'

He shook his head sadly. 'More trouble?' he asked. 'When will you ever learn?'

'It's the breaks, Charlie. Shit happens.'

'So what is it this time?'

'Long story.'

'They always are. Is it to do with Laura's death?'

I nodded.

'I never knew why you married her.'

'Because she was there. She was a challenge. And if I hadn't, I wouldn't have Judith, would I?'

'That's a point.'

'So can you help me?'

'You're not having anything off the lot, that's for sure. Let me think.' He paused for a second. 'Got it,' he said, took out his mobile and punched in a number. 'Jeff,' he said after a moment. 'That ringer you got garaged up: what's the lowest price?'

A pause.

'Too much. I'll give you a monkey.'

Another pause.

'Done deal. Right. Get it over here.'

Another pause.

'No. Tuesday fuckin' fortnight. What do you think? Get it over here now.' And he cut off the call. 'Pillock,' he said. 'It's not far. Give him half an hour.'

Thirty-five minutes later a blue Rover 600 slowed down and stopped outside the car lot. Charlie went over, had a short conversation with the driver, a sandy-haired individual, who then got out of the car and walked off without a backward glance.

Charlie came back with the keys. 'That's five hundred you owe me,' he said. Before I could reply, he stopped me. 'Don't worry,' he said. 'I'll put it on your bill.'

'Cheers, mate,' I replied. 'I won't forget this.'

'Don't worry. I won't let you.'

21

Thursday afternoon

I took the car and headed east. There was only one person I knew who might be able to help. He wasn't exactly a friend, but then he wasn't exactly an enemy. Or at least he hadn't been the last time we met. The motor was OK. A bit sluggish, but it'd do. The tank was almost empty so I filled it up at a garage in Dulwich and had another snort in the freezing-cold gents'. The life of Riley, or what?

When I left the garage I caught the news on Capital on the half-hour. The lead story was the triple murder at the hotel. My name wasn't mentioned, but the newscaster said that a man was being sought in connection, followed by a pretty good description of me. But then it was a pretty good description of at least ten thousand other geezers in London. I knew that more would follow.

It was snowing again when I got to Deptford, and the sky had an evil yellow cast as dusk set in early. I drove the car on to the notorious Lion Estate and parked it between two others by one of the high-rise blocks. Before I got out of the Rover, I transferred Latimer's Colt to the glove compartment. The other two guns I kept on me.

I went into the entrance hall and climbed four flights of stairs to the flat I remembered and wondered if the tenant would still be in occupancy, or doing bird at Her Majesty's pleasure.

The door to the flat was protected by metal, like the last time I'd visited, and I hammered on it with my fist. After a minute a slot opened and I saw a pair of brown eyes looking me up and down. 'Nick Sharman,' I said. 'To see the Darkman. I've been here before.'

'I remember you, mon,' said the owner of the eyes. 'Hold on.'

The door opened with a screech and I saw the huge black man I'd seen on my previous visit about fifteen months before.

'Come in,' he said.

'I'm carrying,' I said. 'But let's not do the full body search this time.'

I pulled out the two guns I was holding and handed them over. 'That's all, and I'll have them back,' I said.

'Cool runnin',' said the dude. 'No problem.'

'Is he at home?' I asked.

'Sure. I'll let him know you're calling.'

I waited in the hall whilst the black man went into the living room. A moment later he was back and said, 'He'll see you, mon.'

I went into the room, which was hot and dimly lit, and the Darkman was sitting on his throne just like the last time. Only now he didn't look as well as I remembered, his black skin waxy and tight on his skull. There was drug paraphernalia littered about again too, but this time there were several crack pipes and Coke cans punctured with ballpoint pen barrels, held tight by wads of Sellotape. Darkman was going down a different road. A bad road full of potholes that would eventually lead to his death.

The TV was on in one corner, tuned into the news.

'Sharman,' he said. 'Long time. You're famous, man!' He gestured at the TV. 'You on *London Today*! Cool. Killing cops, man. I take my hat off to you. Five-oh all runnin' round like chickens with their heads cut off.'

'Shit,' I said. 'Did they mention my name?'

'Sure. And a nice photo. And straight away you turn up here. Coincidence, or what?'

'Not entirely. And I didn't kill no cops.'

'But you come here armed to the teeth. What should a boy think about that?'

'Whatever you like. But I didn't kill anybody.'

'So what can I do for you, big-time desperado? I'll be honoured to help!'

'I'm looking for someone,' I said. 'And people he hangs out with.'

'Who?'

'A Yank. Jefferson Parker from New York. His mates are Yardies.'

'Who the fuck are Yardies, man? You've been reading too many newspapers.'

'Don't dis me, Darkman,' I said. 'I didn't come upstream on a lettuce leaf. Yardies exist. They killed those coppers.'

'Heavy duty, man. You don't want to mess with those boys and girls.'

'They're messing with me. And talking of girls, where's Marsha?'

Marsha had been the Darkman's woman the last time I called.

His lip curled. 'She gone, man. Quit on me. I had her striped. No one leaves without my say-so.'

'It must've been your new-man attitudes that got to her. Or was it the crack? That's bad stuff.'

'Get you high, though, man.'

'So are you going to help me?' I asked.

'The brothers won't like it.'

'That's their problem. My problem is more pressing. If Old

Bill gets me, they're going to lock me up and throw away the key. I've got a reputation and this morning didn't help it.'

'What did this dude Parker do?'

'He was grassing up his mates, from what I can gather. He'd been arrested in New York and the coppers turned him round. He sold out his pals in exchange for going into witness protection.'

'Over here?'

'Here, there and everywhere. He was going abundance on everyone he could think of.'

'And now they've got him.'

'Either that or he double-crossed the coppers himself. It doesn't matter. There are three policemen dead. Two from America and one from the Met. Plus another couple murdered in that plane crash in Chicago the other day. Not to mention the other four hundred-odd civilians who got caught in the crossfire.' I didn't mention Laura, Louis and David. 'It's fucking heavy-duty, Darkman, and it looks like I've been voted the boy most likely to carry the can back home.'

'And you want me to get involved? You gotta be joking.'

'It's no joke.'

'It is from where I'm sitting.'

22

'I thought you said you'd be honoured to help,' I said.

'That was before I knew what you wanted.'

'Can you do anything for me?'

'I can let you have a blow.'

'No, man. I got my own.'

'Then you're sorted.'

I suddenly had a brainwave. 'Then you're not interested in the money?'

'What money?'

'The money Parker was carrying.'

'How much?'

'Christ knows, but a lot,' I lied. Shit. Right then I'd've sworn the Pope was a Jew to get some slack.

'How do you know?' Darkman asked with a greedy gleam in his yellow-rimmed eyes.

'I saw it,' I lied again. 'A big caseful. Some kind of profit from a deal in New York.' I was on a roll and began to elaborate. 'American currency. Thousand-dollar bills, I think.'

Darkman chewed on that for a minute. 'Maybe,' he said. 'Maybe I might be able to come up with something.'

Funny that I knew he was going to say that.

'How about a beer to be going on with?' I asked. 'My throat's as dry as a bone.'

It was too. I knew that I was in deep trouble already, and lying to Darkman wasn't going to help. Well, maybe for a bit. But when he found out that I was having him on . . . Well, the old sewage was going to hit the fan big time.

He went and told his minder to get me a Red Stripe, which

I drank in the living room, and had another line of coke, whilst he went off and made a couple of calls.

He was back within fifteen minutes and said, 'Maybe, man. Just maybe I found out something.'

'That was quick.'

'The thought of much ready cash can have that effect.'

Yeah, I thought. But what happens when the thought turns out to be pie in the sky?

'But, of course, if you lying . . .'

For a minute I thought he was reading my mind.

'What me, man,' I said. 'Perish the thought.'

23

'But first,' he said, 'we gotta find you somewhere to stay. You're too hot to be wandering round town on your own.'

'How about here?'

'No, man, I don't think so. What would nine-nine-nine say if they found you here?'

'Shit, would you care? Look around, the place is rotten with dope and weapons. What difference would I make?'

'The difference that might just bring them here. Who knows who saw you come in?'

He had a valid point.

'No, man,' he went on. 'I've got just the place. Perfection. There's food, booze, women and plenty of coke.'

'What is it? The YMCA?'

'Always the humour, Sharman. Don't you take anything seriously?'

'Sure. But you've got to have a laugh, ain'tcha?'

He shook his head and left me alone in the room with another beer, a packet of Silk Cut and the depleted wrap of cocaine.

That time he was gone for maybe fifteen minutes, and when he returned he was wearing a sharp overcoat and carrying a brown suede briefcase. The big black guy was with him, wearing a leather anorak. Obviously time for walkies. In one massive hand the black guy was carrying my brace of guns and he passed them to me. I checked them. They were both still loaded.

'OK,' said Darkman. 'Let's split.'

'Where we going?' I asked.

'To do some business,' he replied.

'I won't ask what kind.'

'I think you already know.'

We went out of the flat and down the stairs when I said I'd take my motor, but Darkman told me I was driving with them. I shrugged. What the hell? I thought, I'll probably never see it again, and retrieved the Colt from it before we walked round to a garage that appeared to be the only one in the block not burnt out, and I said as much.

'No motherfucker's gonna mess with Darkman's stuff,' said the black guy, and opened up the garage door with some gizmo on his keyring, to display a black Mercedes 190 with black bumpers and black windows. 'Discreet,' I said. 'Looks like a drug dealer's motor.'

'So it is,' said Darkman. 'What did you expect us to drive? An Escort van?'

'Just a thought?' I said as the black guy got in, started up the motor and let it drift out of the garage with a muted rumble. 'Where we going?' I repeated.

'Maida Vale, man,' said Darkman as we got in, him riding shotgun and me stretched out on the black leather back seat. 'Nice area.'

'What's there?'

'Pussy farm, man,' said the black geezer. 'Wall-to-wall cunt.'

'Whorehouse,' explained Darkman as if I might not have guessed. 'Have yourself some fun on the firm, and keep your head down.'

'The mind boggles,' I said.

We headed north away from Deptford, crossed the river and went through the West End up to Maida Vale. The black geezer steered the car expertly through the traffic and parked outside an imposing mansion block.

We left him in the motor and Darkman and I went to the main entrance. It was locked, with an entryphone stuck on the wall. He did the business and a vaguely female voice squawked at us, and then he whispered something into the mike. The door buzzed and we were inside.

The flat we wanted was on the first floor. I would've walked but Darkman insisted on waiting for the cranky old lift. When it finally arrived we squeezed in and he hit the button. The hall outside the lift was wide, carpeted in purple and very quiet. We walked to a door marked 108 and he rapped with his knuckles on the wood. A few seconds later it was answered by a short, good-looking redhead in a miniskirt, black nylons and a thin T-shirt top. She wore nothing underneath it and her breasts were clearly visible, nipples erect. 'Baby,' she said when she saw us, and I guessed she wasn't referring to me.

'Hi, Angie,' he said.

He introduced Angie and me by our Christian names and we went inside. There was a big geezer sitting in a chair just inside the door. He had the *Standard* on a small table beside him next to the ashtray. He looked at us in a deadpan way but said and did nothing else.

Angie led us down another hall and into the living room of the flat that had been converted into a bar and waiting room for the punters. The blinds were drawn, two other young women were sitting on a sofa talking, and an older woman sat on a stool behind the bar. Paul McCartney and Wings was on the stereo and racing was on the box, with the sound turned down, on a shelf in the corner.

All in all it was pretty depressing. But sometimes I think I get too easily depressed these days, what with one thing and another.

The older woman stood up when we entered, and Angie clapped her hands at the two girls on the sofa. 'Come on, you lot,' she said. 'Look alive! We have guests.'

The two girls got up and sashayed over. Angie said, 'Beer?' Darkman and I both nodded and the older woman set up six bottles and knocked the tops off each.

We sat down on the stools in front of the bar and Darkman set his briefcase on the counter. Angie stood close to him and the other two girls made a beeline for me. I got a brunette of about twenty in a low-cut black dress and a girl with slightly lighter hair and similar outfit, but this time in red.

The brunette reached for her drink, bumping me as she did so, and said, 'You look sad.'

I looked at her and sipped at the neck of my bottle. 'I am sad,' I replied.

'You don't have to be.'

'Don't I?'

'No. I'm here now.'

'And you can help?'

'I've done it before.'

'Not with me.'

'True. But we could have fun trying.'

'Another time, maybe. I'm with him and he's here on business. Another kind of business,' I added.

'I know that,' said the girl. 'I'm not stupid,' and turned to her friend.

But you're here, I thought, but said nothing. I was there, too. Work it out.

Darkman drank some of his beer, then went over to the sofa with Angie, put the briefcase on his knee and opened it. I couldn't see the contents because the top was in front of me, but it didn't matter as he pulled out a plastic baggie, fat with all sorts. But not the liquorice kind.

Angie had a close squint then pulled a wad of notes from the waistband of her skirt and they did a swap. Darkman closed the case and whispered something to her. She looked at me, shrugged and whispered something back. Darkman came back to the bar and motioned the older woman over. They had a whispered conversation too, and this time it was her that gave me a long look before nodding.

Darkman grinned and moved down the bar towards me. 'You're staying,' he said. 'It's all arranged. You've got to choose one of those two.' He indicated the girls that had almost joined me.

'What?' I said. 'I dunno . . .'

'Do it,' he said. 'Fuck me, man! It's all free. I'm taking care of the bill.'

'You're too kind,' I said. 'OK, I'll take her.' I nodded in the direction of the brunette who'd spoken to me. At least we'd had some kind of relationship, however brief.

'Fine,' he said. 'Yo, Annette! Get your fine botty over here. You got a new boyfriend.'

24

'Lucky me,' she said, as she came back into our sphere of influence. 'Just when I thought the whole day was going to be a waste.'

I had to smile. I had been a bit of an arsehole, after all. 'Sorry about before,' I said. 'My day hasn't been that great either.' Understatement, or what?

'Is that right? I am sorry.'

Obviously I'd trodden on a pet corn with my previous comment. Perhaps she was a distress counsellor beneath the slap.

'Another drink?' I said, to break the mood.

'Sure. A large brandy.'

I looked at Darkman's face. He wasn't happy. 'I'll pay for the booze,' I said, as I ordered a round for the house. 'We don't want you getting into the red.'

Whilst the woman behind the bar was getting our drinks, I dragged Darkman to one side. 'Do they know I'm Britain's most wanted?' I asked.

'They know you're in trouble. Don't worry about it. They're used to it here.'

'I'll be in bigger trouble if one of them sees the news and grasses me up.'

'Don't worry, they won't. They like living.' He had an evil leer on his face as he spoke, and I believed him. But you never know what people will do.

'Famous last words,' I said.

'Listen. You're safe here. Take my word.'

'I've got no choice, have I?'

'Not a lot.'

'OK. But not too long, eh?'

'Not at the prices they're charging me for your bed and board, believe me.'

'And not just bed and board by the sounds of it.'

'This ain't a fucking hotel, man. They've only got so many rooms. You've got to share. Sorry ... What the fuck am I saying? How hard is it going to be, staying with her?'

'Depends on how good she is.'

'You're a filthy bastard, Sharman.'

Whilst we'd been talking I'd noticed the older woman giving Annette the SP. She didn't look too pleased, but on the other hand she hadn't slashed her wrists, so I guessed every-thing would work out. That is, as long as one of the girls didn't check my mug on TV and decide to turn me in.

We went back and Annette gave me a closer look. 'Seems you're staying with me,' she said.

'A minder,' I replied. 'I've always wanted one.'

25

When he'd finished his beer, Darkman split. 'I'll be in touch later,' he said at the off. 'Don't leave the place. There's everything you want here.'

'Apart from the bastards who killed those coppers.' And Laura too, but I didn't say that. That could wait.

'Don't worry about the filth. There's too many of them as it is.'

But who do you call when someone's nicked the video? A drug dealer? Probably. But only to buy the sodding thing back.

'Sure,' I said. But that wasn't the way I felt.

After he'd gone, I went back to join Annette. 'Want to see where you're staying?' she said.

'Sure.'

She took me out of the bar, down the hall to another room. Inside, it was sizeable, the walls painted peach, with a high ceiling and two big windows looking out over the service area at the back of the flats. Outside the window was a metal walkway and a fire escape leading up and down. Useful, I thought.

The room was split into two by a divider. One half was the sleeping and business part, with a large double bed covered in cuddly toys, and a wardrobe and washbasin. In the other was a sofa, coffee table, stereo, TV and video and a bookcase crammed with paperbacks. It was warm and perfumed and she drew thick drapes over the windows.

'Nice,' I said.

'I have to live here too.' And I started to feel sad again. This time for her, and that was dangerous.

To break *that* mood I took the two automatics out of my coat pockets and the Colt that was tucked into my belt, and threw them on the counterpane.

'Jesus,' she said. 'Who are you?'

'That doesn't matter. But I know that you know that the police think I've been a naughty boy. But I haven't. It's a long story that doesn't concern you. But I can be. And I will if anyone here thinks it'd be a good idea to give them a buzz.'

81

'Not me,' she said, glancing at the guns from the corner of her eye. 'I'm like the three wise monkeys all rolled into one.'

'That's good, Annette,' I said. 'Very good. You remember that and you'll be fine and we'll get along great. But forget it for a moment and I promise you'll be living in a world of pain you never knew existed. You clear on that?'

She said nothing, so I grabbed her wrist and twisted it hard until she cried out softly.

'I asked if you were clear on that?' I hated behaving like that, but I had to show her what I was capable of. Or maybe wasn't. But I hoped neither of us would be forced to find out.

She nodded and I saw tears in her eyes. 'Now how many of you live here?' I asked.

'Five of us,' she said, rubbing her arm. 'Including May. It's a massive flat.'

'May?'

'The boss. The woman behind the bar.'

'What about the heavy on the door?'

'There's three of them. They work shifts. They don't live here.'

'Fine. Tell me about the place.'

'What about it?'

'The layout.'

'You saw the bar. That's where we sit when we're working, but not . . . working. If you see what I mean.'

'I see.'

'Go down the hall and there's four more bedrooms like this, two bathrooms, a separate loo, and at the side a big kitchen. That's all there is to it.'

'Good. See, it's no problem, Annette, is it? We can be pals for as long as I'm here. Which I hope won't be long.'

I could tell from her face that she seconded that motion.

'There's no need to be horrible to me,' she said. 'I won't tell on you.'

'I know you won't, love. The spade I came in with can turn nasty if provoked. Nastier than me. And I'm bad enough.'

'I know all about him.'

'Good. Now I'm going to need some things.'

'What sort of things.'

'Toothbrush, razor, shaving foam. Some socks and underwear.'

'There's a Marks not far and a big Boots.'

'Great. You can do me a bit of shopping this afternoon. But make sure you go to the shops. *Capeesh?*'

'I understand.'

'Then we'll both get along famously.'

26

Thursday afternoon/Thursday evening

'Do you want to?' she said, looking at the bed where the guns still lay.

I knew what she meant. 'No thanks, love,' I said. 'I'm not in the mood right now.' After what I'd seen that morning I didn't know when I'd be in the mood again. 'Tell me about the other girls who stay here.'

'There's Angie, and the other girl you saw, Dot. Then there's Emily. She's got a punter.'

'So you're quiet.'

'It's the time of year. All the johns are getting it for free at the office party.'

Shit, I'd forgotten about Christmas. And Judith. I needed to phone her.

'You go shopping,' I said. 'I need to make a call.'

'There's no phone in here . . . It's in the bar.'

'I've got a mobile.'

I fished in my pocket for one of the fifties I'd liberated from Parker's room and gave it to her. 'Socks to fit shoe size ten. Black. Three pairs. Medium T-shirt and shorts. White. The same. A shirt. Oxford cotton, button-down would be good. Any colour. Sixteen-and-a-half collar. Extra-long sleeves. And the toilet stuff.'

'I remember.'

'Good girl. And not a word. Remember that too.'

'I will.'

'Great. So off you go.'

She got a black double-breasted coat out of the wardrobe and put it on, then left.

I took out the wrap and did up a line on the coffee table, then lit a cigarette and wished for a beer. But I wasn't going back to the bar. Who knew who'd be there? Instead I took out the mobile I'd taken from Latimer, switched it on and keyed in Jane's home number.

She answered on the third ring. 'Nick,' I said.

'What the hell have you been up to now? It's all over the news.'

'It wasn't me Jane. I was set up.'

'Again?'

'Again. Is Judith there?'

'Of course.'

'Then let me speak to her.'

84

The handset went down hard and after a second or two Judith came on. 'Daddy,' she said, 'how come it's always you?'

'Just lucky, I guess. You know it wasn't me.'

''Course.'

'That's one of the best things about you: you always believe me, no matter what.'

'Where are you?'

'Better you don't know. But I'm safe.'

'Are you going to be all right?'

'Sure I am,' I said with more conviction than I felt.

'Because I don't think I can go through this again. Not you. You're all I've got left.'

I felt a lump in my throat. 'Don't cry, baby,' I said.

'I'm not going to. I'm all cried out.'

I felt like a complete failure.

'Judith,' I said, 'I promise you faithfully I'll get this sorted. Christmas dinner, remember? Am I still invited?'

'I remember. Of course you are. It wouldn't be the same without you. And I've got you a nice present.' But her voice sounded old and lost, and I don't think she expected me.

'And *your* present,' I said, remembering the parcel I'd hidden in the bottom of my wardrobe back in the flat; the one I was going to give her before she left for the States. 'You've got to have that on Christmas Day. It's important.'

'That'll be nice.'

'It's something you want.' It was a pair of leather boots with rollerblades attached, and they'd cost me one and a half at Lilly-whites. She *was* going to get them, too. On Christmas Day if I had to kill to get them there. But that was what I was afraid of. 'Trust me, darling,' I said. 'I've not let you down yet.'

That was a laugh.

'I trust you, Daddy. And I love you.'

85

'I've got to go now, sweetheart. I'll see you on Monday, if not before.'

Four days. Four days to get everything copacetic. Well, we'd see.

'Goodbye, Daddy,' she said. 'Do you want to speak to Auntie Jane?'

'I don't think so. Give her my love.'

'I will.'

'Bye.' And I cut off the call.

Then the phone rang.

'Shit,' I said aloud, and nearly dropped the bloody thing. It felt red-hot in my hand. For a second I was tempted to answer it, but resisted and turned it off instead. Surely they couldn't trace its location, could they? That would be just great.

After all that, I needed a beer even more and I was starting to get hungry, but still wouldn't leave the safety of Annette's room.

I went to the sofa, sat down and lit a cigarette. There was a knock on the door. I stood up, grabbed the Colt, went over and opened it a fraction. I didn't really expect Old Bill to be so polite, but you never knew. Instead, the woman from behind the bar was standing there with a tray of sandwiches, a vacuum flask, a cup, saucer, sugar bowl and, best of all, two bottles of Becks in an ice bucket with a glass. 'I thought you might want something to eat,' she said. 'Can I come in?'

'You're amazing,' I said, opened the door all the way and let her in.

'I'm May,' she said coolly, with a slight Liverpool accent, eyeing the pistol. 'And I hope you won't have to use that.'

'I know,' I said. 'Annette told me. Sorry about the gun. Force of habit.'

'Normally I wouldn't let you in here with it, but I owe Darkman plenty. He saw off some very nasty people for me a while ago.'

'I'm glad,' I said. 'Otherwise it'd be a cardboard box in Waterloo for me tonight, and it's no weather for it.'

'He told me you were OK. I hope he was right.'

'I didn't do it, if that's what you mean.'

'That's exactly what I mean, Mr Sharman. It's not a great photo.'

'You've seen the TV?'

'And the later editions of the *Standard*. You're a popular man.'

'Listen. If you don't want me here I'd rather just go than have half the Met come round with semi-automatic weapons.'

'They won't hear about it from me or any of my girls. We're loyal and know when to keep our mouths shut.'

'And the bloke on the door?'

'Him too. Just don't outstay your welcome.'

'I won't, May. I might be gone tonight. Darkman's doing some digging for me to find out who really murdered those people.'

'I believe you, thousands wouldn't. Enjoy your food.'

'I will, May, believe me.'

'And listen. You didn't have to hurt Annette. That was out of order.'

I felt like a shit again. 'I know,' I said. 'I was scared.'

'We're all scared, Mr Sharman. It's the human condition. What we do here isn't exactly legal, you know. We don't want the scuffers round mob-handed any more than you do. Just remember that Annette's merchandise, my merchandise, and I don't want her damaged. If she is you'll pay, and pay heavily.'

Merchandise. So much for sisters under the skin.

'I'll remember that, May,' I assured her.

'Be sure you do.'

And she left me to my snack. But I'd lost my appetite and just poured myself a beer.

27

Not long after, Annette came back. She had a couple of plastic shopping bags with her, and a small black carry-all. 'Thought you might need this,' she said. 'For your stuff.'

I could've wept.

'Thanks,' I said.

'I've got your change.'

'Keep it. And listen. I didn't mean to scare you before. I overreacted. I'm in trouble. Very deep trouble. It tends to darken the mood.'

She smiled. 'I know,' she said. 'My dad was in trouble a lot too. He took it out on all of us.'

'But I don't,' I said. 'As a rule. It's not my game. It won't happen again. Promise.'

'Good. Oh, I got you this.' She rummaged around in the M&S bag and brought out the *Standard*. My photo was on the front. I looked like the Yorkshire Ripper. Christ knows where they'd got that one, but it wouldn't get me a part in *Baywatch*.

'Cheers,' I said and scanned the story. It was pretty much as I'd imagined it would be.

I tossed the paper on the coffee table and said, 'Fancy a sandwich?'

There was another knock on the door then. The room was getting like Piccadilly Circus. Annette looked alarmed, but not, I imagine, as alarmed as me. 'Get it,' I said, pulling out the Colt.

'Who is it?' she called, before opening the door.

'Emily,' said a voice from the other side.

'It's Emily,' she told me.

'I got that,' I replied.

'Shall I . . . ?'

'Go on then. I might as well meet the whole gang.' Christ, I thought, putting the gun away. This never happens in Richard Widmark movies when he's on the lam.

Annette opened the door to admit a tiny, beautiful Chinese girl in a flower-patterned dress, high at the neck and split up both sides to expose good legs. She wore very high heels, but still couldn't've been more than five-one or two. 'This is Emily,' Annette said. 'Emily Cheng.'

This was getting more like Open Day at a girls' school by the minute.

'Nick,' I said, assuming Emily knew as much about me as everyone else seemed to, and I wondered when it would stop. Hopefully before the SPG came bursting through the door.

But where else could I go?

'Hello,' said Emily. 'I'm on the cadge.'

Liar, I thought. You're just nosy.

'Have you got any tampons, Annie?' she said. 'I've come on. And I've been just too busy to get to the shops.'

'You'll have a few days off now.'

'Suppose so. Unless I stick to blow-jobs.'

'It'll give you a break over Christmas,' said Annette, going to her bag.

89

'Yeah,' said Emily. 'And I was ready to kill, with PMT.' She looked at me. 'Sorry.'

She knew.

'That's all right,' I said. 'Emily. That's a nice name.'

'Thanks. My mum was English. Dad was Cantonese. And I've heard all the jokes about chop suey.'

'Sure you have. I wasn't going to make any. But there's a good one about twenty number six.'

She laughed and stuck out her tongue at that.

The place *was* like a girls' school.

'He's nice,' she said to Annette. 'Oops, I'm leaking. See you later.' And she scampered out of the room clutching a box of Tampax.

28

Annette and I watched the evening news. My picture was on it again, the story second only to another disaster for the royal family. The third story was about a big jewel robbery in Bond Street.

I sent her to the bar after that for cigarettes, more beers, a bottle of JD, ice, lemon, and half a dozen cans of coke.

'You want anything to go with that?' she asked on her return.

'Like?'

'Darkman made a delivery this morning. We've got everything.'

'Like?'

'Dope, coke, Es, crack, uppers, downers. The whole nine yards.'

'And what's your pleasure?'

'I like a little draw, and some charlie sometimes.'

'But not crack.'

'No way. I've seen some of the girls who go for that. They don't last long.'

'So who *is* it for?'

'Punters, mostly.'

'Fair enough. I could do with a joint.'

'Great,' she said, and showed me a parcel of grass she'd put on the tray with the drinks. 'Skunk. This'll do your head in.'

I was quite prepared to believe it.

I knew I should stay alert, but I also knew I wouldn't sleep after the day I'd had without a little something. And who the hell knew when Darkman would get in touch, or even if he would at all? And what would happen if Old Bill turned up at 3 a.m. and I was out of it on strong grass and booze? Frankly, if they did, by then I probably wouldn't care. All that ran through my mind as Annette loaded up a three-skinner with just a little tobacco from one of my Silk Cuts and what looked like an eighth of an ounce of pure, green, odorous skunk.

Who the hell could read the future? And if we could, wouldn't we just open our wrists at the knowledge?

So when the joint was lit, I gratefully accepted it and took several deep drags as I lay back on the sofa.

Jesus, but skunk is strong. Almost psychedelic in its effects, and after only a few seconds the lights in the room took on halos and I felt bombed out, big time.

Then there was another knock on the door. I licked my dry lips and picked up the Colt that felt as heavy as a brick.

It was May. 'Darkman's been on,' she said, and her voice seemed to come from miles away.

'Does he want to talk to me?' I slurred.

She shook her head, and it seemed to take minutes. 'No,' she replied. 'He told me to tell you to hang on in here. He'll be in touch in the morning. He said he might have something sorted.'

Sorted, I thought. Just like me. 'Thanks, May?' I said, my voice echoing in my head. 'That's great.'

'Have a good night,' she said. 'See you in the morning.' And she gently closed the door.

'You look done in,' said Annette. 'Want to go to bed?'

'I dunno, babe,' I said. 'Perhaps I should just stay here.'

I saw her pout. 'It's all paid for,' she said. 'No one's coming to disturb us.'

She got up and sashayed across the carpet to the bed area, where she stood with her back to me and pulled her dress over her head. She was wearing hold-ups, little black panties that almost disappeared up the crack of her arse and a thin black bra. She took everything off, still with her back to me, and pulled on a short raspberry-coloured silk nightie that she took from the wardrobe. It hardly covered her cheeks and had old-fashioned lace around the bottom. When she turned back to me it flared slightly to show me the patch of dark hair between her thighs. 'Come on,' she said. 'Be a devil.'

I thought of her warm body and the soft bed and began to unbutton my shirt, and wondered if I'd actually make it as far as the mattress.

29

Friday morning

I woke up at about three and crawled out of Annette's rumpled bed. I pulled on my jeans and shirt, sat on the sofa in the faint light that crept through a crack in the curtains from the lamps in the street outside, lit a cigarette and poured a glass of Jack. I drank it straight without ice or mix and it tasted like medicine. Maybe that's just what I needed: a taste of my own medicine.

Annette slept on.

I sat there until seven, smoking and sipping until she woke up. It was still dark. 'Nick? Where are you?' she said.

'Right here, honey.'

'Are you all right?'

'Never better,' I lied.

'Do you want to come back to bed?'

'No.'

'Please. That was good.'

'Was it?' I'd already forgotten.

''Course it was.'

'I bet you say that to all the boys.'

'No. I mean it.'

She got up then and came over to join me. She slipped on the silk nightie again as she came. She snuggled up close and it felt as if she were dressed in water. 'Come on, Nick. Just a quickie. It'll be fun.'

'Don't you get enough of this at work? Or is it work?'

'This is purely pleasure.'

'You certainly know how to get round a man.'

'Just this man, I hope.'

'You're doing it again.'

'Am I?' she asked innocently, got up and went behind the divider, and like a dog I followed her.

We stayed in bed until it got light, late on, maybe eight-thirty, quarter to nine. Then she got up, put on a robe and went and made breakfast. I managed some toast and coffee before I went down for a shave, cleaned my teeth, used the toilet and got dressed. When I got back to the room, Annette said, 'Darkman's been on. He wants to see you at ten. He's got some news.'

Just as well, I thought, as she had GMTV on, and I was still a featured attraction on the news segment.

I sat and smoked and watched her get herself together until May came and told me that Darkman was waiting in the bar.

It was empty except for him and I sat on the stool next to his. 'What's occurring?' I asked.

'I found your friend,' he said.

'He's no friend of mine.'

'Whatever. I tracked him down.'

'And?'

'And he's not a very nice guy.'

'I could've told you that.'

'And you're not the only face looking for him.'

'I think I could've worked that one out too. The coppers must be after him after what happened at the hotel.'

'And some of his old associates.'

'And you and me and Uncle Tom Cobley and all.'

'Just about. But his associates want him most. And they want to meet you too.'

'Really.'

'Really.'

'Cosy.'

'Cosy,' he agreed. 'Then there's the money.'

Thin ice time. 'Yeah?'

'Yeah. His associates didn't know about that. That's one of the reasons they want to see you.'

Fuck, I thought. I could be up shit creek without a paddle. But what's a boy to do? 'Don't ask me, man,' I said. 'I only told you what I saw. It could've been snide for all I know.'

'I hope not, for your sake.'

And I hoped I looked more confident than I felt. But it was my only chance. I had to find Parker and find him soon. After all, I had promised Judith.

'Where and when?' I asked.

'Tonight. Eleven o'clock, Victoria station concourse.'

'Jesus Christ, man . . .'

'That's the way they want it.'

'OK, OK. How will I find them?'

'Don't worry. They'll find you. Then I'll find the lot of you. Just be sure that money exists. Otherwise I'll make sure your clock's stopped. And if I don't, others will.'

And with that, he put on his coat and left.

And with that, I had my first drink of the day.

30

Friday evening

I spent the rest of the day with Annette, doing what you do with a free brass, and counting my bullets. There were fourteen in all, spread over the three guns.

Then around ten I bade her a fond farewell, put my few things, including Isaac's .45 into the black bag, distributed the other two guns about my person and headed towards Victoria, and my appointment with Darkman's contacts.

I dumped Latimer's mobile into the first garbage bin I saw on the way.

Of course, being that time of the year, there wasn't a sodding lobster around with its light on, so in the end I walked to Edgware Road and caught a bus. This sort of thing never happened to Mike Hammer.

Victoria at eleven o'clock on the last Friday night before Christmas. Hell is a city very much like that.

The streets around the station were packed with humanity, if you could call it that. Inhumanity more like. A movable feast of horror. Every low-life, scumbag, hustler, mutant, conman, ponce, nonce, drifter, thief, beggar and arsehole of both sexes – and maybe more – in the universe, seemed to have made a beeline for the area.

Pond life. Pod people. So far down the food chain they made amoebae look sophisticated.

And it was cold. Bone-numbingly cold. As I walked from

the bus stop I gathered Parker's coat closely around myself and shivered.

The station itself stank of piss and vomit, and the tiled floor was slick with slime. There were people with their shoelaces undone, their flies undone, and their trousers wet with urine. And others talking to themselves, or the demons who haunted them, as if they were alone. Everyone seemed to be drunk, and eating some unspeakable takeaway, or drinking from bottles or tinnies.

Outside, where a dank yellow mist stinking of petrol and diesel hung over London, obscuring the stars; where a few taxis and buses rattled around the terminus, and the queues for cabs were a hundred yards long and four deep, black snow rimmed the kerbs and gutters. But street people still squatted there, holding up paper cups for any money forthcoming from the crowds rushing past. Sometimes these street people got the odd coin, but more often they got insulted, pissed on, assaulted, or worse. But still they sat there like ragged crows rattling the change they had managed to collect from the pissed-up mug punters.

The pubs were just starting to chuck out and office boys were trying to get their fingers into secretaries' G-strings to show their undying love and release the tightness in their bollocks. People who were old enough to know better were exchanging French kisses with the enthusiasm of teenagers, before they caught the last train home to the spouse.

Zeitgeist à gogo.

I hated being there. The place gave me the creeps, big time. Predatory eyes were everywhere. Predatory eyes looking for some chicken on the run from an unhappy home searching for the streets paved with gold. Either sex. It didn't matter. Both boys and girls had a warm and damp orifice where some pervert somewhere would like to lodge his dick. Predatory eyes looking for a mark to rob or con or generally fuck over for his or her Christmas bonus. And other eyes looking for a certain individual who'd had his name and face plastered all over the media for the last thirty-six hours. And they were the eyes I feared the most.

And it was noisy. Car alarms going off outside and the sound of the human race at play, screaming at the dying of the day. Shouting out their Merry Christmases to friends and even perfect strangers as if they meant it, all competing with the Carpenters' greatest hits, muzak-style, that was dribbling out of one set of speakers and the train announcements that were booming out of another.

So there they were, sports fans. Human filth one and all. And I wasn't much better. Or maybe I was even worse than the worst of them.

31

Friday night

But at least I was armed. Fourteen bullets I'd counted, let dribble through my fingers and put back in their magazines and chambers. Thirteen for thirteen of the revellers, leaving one for me. That'd make a good story to mull over the next day over the eggs and bacon.

But such morbid thoughts for holiday time, and they evaporated when someone tapped me on the shoulder and said, 'Sharman'.

I nearly jumped out of my skin, and one hand went inside my coat to the pistol tucked down my jeans close to my balls. I half turned and a black geezer with dreadlocks long and tight enough to clean a lavatory bowl, wearing a dark, single-breasted mac over a track suit, was standing behind me. 'Relax, mon,' he said with a white, gappy-toothed grin. 'We all brothers here.'

'You'll be a dead fucking brother if you come up behind me like that again, *mon*,' I hissed.

'Be cool, mon,' said the spade. 'We hear you one chilly dude. Come along-a-me. There's some folks want to see you. We gonna party, bro.'

Shit, I thought. Just what I need. A fucking party. But I let him lead me out of the concourse down to Wilton Street where a car was parked facing south.

Of course it was a Beemer. A silver Alpine with fat, alloy wheels, low-profile tyres and all sorts of skirts and shit attached. I knew it was our motor, as the sound of amplified jungle could be heard two blocks away.

'Discreet,' I said. 'You know I'm carrying.'

'Us too, mon. Browning Hi-Power. The only guns for the only ones.'

Shit, the geezer was stoned to the bone. Or pretending to be.

There was one guy in the car, behind the wheel. Another spade, another haircut. This time a high-top fade with a marijuana leaf carved in the back.

I saw that as the interior light winked on when the first one opened the door for me to get in.

'Turn the fucking music down, will you?' I almost screamed as the driver slapped the motor into gear and took off like a scalded cat once we were both inside.

He looked over his shoulder at me with a scowl as he narrowly missed a garbage truck, but did as I asked.

'Cool,' said the first guy. 'Dis is Marcus. Me Harold. You Nick, correct?'

'On the button,' I said. 'Where we going?'

'The independent state of Brixton,' he replied, pronouncing it *Brix-tun*. 'See me guv'nor.'

We screamed into the independent state about fifteen minutes later and diddled around the back streets into one of those big squares full of huge detached houses that show what Brixton was like pre-war, before the council knocked the shit out of it and built vile high-rises for the plebs. We drew up in front of the biggest house.

'We 'ere,' said Harold and hopped out, and I crawled out after him. He was young, see. Maybe only twenty-two or three, and I wasn't.

Harold indicated that our journey was over, and Marcus took off to pastures new in the BMW with a roar from the engine, a screech of rubber and a blast from his stereo system.

The house seemed to have every light inside on full and when we went up the path, strong security spots lit the way for us.

'Big electricity bill,' I said.

''E can afford it,' said Harold proudly.

We climbed the stone steps flanked with concrete lions worn almost smooth by time and weather, and Harold banged on the knocker.

After a moment the door was answered by another lemonade, also in a track suit. This one grinned too, to show more gold than Bond Street, and ushered us in.

Harold led me down a thickly carpeted hall to a cream-painted door and threw it open.

He stood back to allow me to enter the room beyond, which was dimly lit in contrast with the rest of the house.

It was big, with a high ceiling, and once upon a time, when there was still farmland within walking distance, some rich businessman who lived there with his family and commuted to the City by the newly built Southern Railway would have used it as the dining room, or morning room, or some other sodding room. How times change.

But whoever had it now was also rich. The whole place stank of cash. Hardly what I'd expected.

I'd expected a flat on a council estate like Darkman's. All tacky lino and loud reggae. Instead I got Persian rugs deep enough to hide a small dog; loads of cut-glass and china ornaments, and furniture you'd expect to see on the *Antiques Roadshow*.

'You tooled up?' said Harold when he'd shut the door behind us. I nodded. I'd already told him that.

'Gimme.'

Delicate moment. Should I or shouldn't I? After a second I undid my coat and hauled out the Colt revolver.

Harold accepted it and grinned. 'Lemme see,' he said and frisked me, coming up with the Detonics. 'You like back-up,' he remarked.

'A bird in the hand,' I replied.

'Don't fuck with me, mon,' he said. 'And don't fuck with Mister B.'

And who exactly is Mister B. I wondered, but said nothing.

'Gimme the bag now,' he said.

I passed over the black bag Annette had bought for me, he opened it, rifled through the contents and came up with Isaac's .45. 'Regular Terminator,' he said, grinned, put all the guns inside the bag, zipped it up and hung it over his shoulder by the strap, then went over to a set of massive double doors on the other side of the room, tapped and entered. After a second he came out again and beckoned for me to join him. 'Be cool, mon,' he said. 'Your life depends on it.'

I'd had nicer recommendations.

Harold stood back and let me into the room. It was dark inside. Much darker even than the previous room, and lit mostly by a massive aquarium that seemed to fill one whole wall and swirled with fish of the most amazing colours.

I let my eyes adjust for a second. and saw that beside the tank was a desk, and behind the desk sat a black man in a black suit, wearing sunglasses.

'Mr B., Nick Sharman,' said Harold, and stepped outside closing the door behind him, which made the room even darker.

'Sharman,' said Mr B. in a deep and cultured voice. 'I've heard so much about you. It's a pleasure to meet at last. Do sit down.'

Once again it wasn't what I was expecting.

I saw the silhouette of a chair in front of the desk and sidled over, hoping there was nothing for me to trip over *en route*. There wasn't and I sank into the rich leather upholstery and squinted across the desktop. Mr B. was bald and wide, but it was impossible to figure out how tall. 'You got any light in here?' I asked. 'It's like a bloody tomb.'

I know Harold had told me to be cool. But fuck it. I refused to be intimidated.

'This is how I like it,' said Mr B. 'Get used to it.'

'I'm sure I'll grow to love it. Nice fish.'

'You know about fish?'

'Only with chips and brown sauce.'

'My hobby. My friends.'

'A bit cold, I would've thought.'

'You'd be amazed.'

'But not very cuddly.'

Mr B. laughed then. 'Sharman,' he said. 'I heard you were a crazy fucker. How come we haven't met before?'

'Just lucky, I guess. Do you know where Parker is?'

'In this room *I* ask the questions.'

'Fair enough.'

'Tell me about Parker.'

I told him the story so far. All I left out was the bit about the plane crash and who was on board. If he'd had something to do with blowing it up, I didn't want him to think I might bear a grudge.

When I'd finished he said, 'You want something to drink?'

'I thought you'd never ask. Got any brandy?'

'Remy?'

'Sure.'

He must've had some kind of panic button under the desk because an instant later Harold came through the door behind us.

'Remy, bottle,' rasped Mr B. 'Two glasses.'

Harold vanished again, but I'm almost sure he'd been carrying a gun when he came in.

A minute later he was back swinging a bottle and carrying two brandy balloons in the other hand. He allowed the reflection from the other room to light his way, and I saw that Mr B.'s face was scarred from old wounds or burns. Badly. So that his skin looked as if it had been flayed away from his skull, leaving deep trenches in the flesh. It was horrible, like sitting opposite a corrupting corpse. No wonder he liked to be in the dark. I tried not to react, but even behind the lenses of his glasses I knew that he saw my expression, yet made no comment. Behind him, thick, floor-length curtains covered one entire wall of what I imagined must be windows looking out over the back of the house.

Harold poured two generous measures, left the bottle and went back outside.

'Mind if I smoke?' I asked.

'Sure.'

'Got an ashtray?'

'Next to the bottle.' And sure enough there was one. Clean and empty.

'You?' I asked, taking out my Silk Cut.

'No.'

'So,' I said, when I was smoking and had sipped some of the liquor. 'Do you know where Parker is?'

32

'I thought I said that I asked the questions.'

'Sure you did. But since I arrived I've done nothing but talk. I thought it might be your turn now. A little exchange of information, if you get my drift.'

'I get your drift perfectly. You're not scared of me one little bit, are you?'

I had to laugh. 'Don't you believe it. I'm terrified! And I could never trust anyone who wouldn't be, in a situation like this.'

'And you'd be right not to. More brandy?'

'This is not exactly what I expected,' I said.

'Of course not. You expected a cockroach-infested slum full

of young men in bobble hats. But we're not all like that, although some are. We can be as civilized as the best of you. Often much more so. Our culture goes back to a time when this cold little island was populated by nothing more than savages. You should remember that.'

'Yes please,' I said and he poured me a decent measure. My eyes were almost accustomed to the dark by then, and I could see that indeed it looked as if Mr B. had been badly burned at some time in his life. 'So are you going to let me in on the plot?' I asked.

'OK,' he said. 'Parker was liberated from his hotel by some bad people.' Even with his black bins on in the gloom he saw the look on my face. He must've had the eyes of a cat. 'Believe me, Mr Sharman, in all this we're the good guys. Or as good as you're going to get.'

'I believe you,' I said, remembering Harold's warning that my life might depend on my behaviour, but didn't add, thousands wouldn't.

'In doing so they killed three police officers.'

'Not according to the newspapers and TV. According to them I'm suspect number one in that particular incident.'

'Just a ploy, Mr Sharman. They are aware that you didn't do it.'

'How do you know?'

'I have some friends in high places. Expensive friends. It costs me a lot of money to stay *au fait* with events.'

'So why me?'

'You've got a chequered past, Mr Sharman. You're the perfect patsy.'

'Terrific. But why?'

'Because they don't know if Parker went of his own free will or under coercion. They don't want to panic these bad people into killing Parker. He has some information that would be useful to the filth,' Mr B. went on. 'And possibly hurtful to me.'

I can imagine, I thought.

'And where does Darkman come in?'

'Our mutual friend? Black trash. But even trash has its uses from time to time. According to him Parker has a large amount of money, which only you seem to have seen. This is not what I was led to expect. Nor was I expecting Parker to be in a room full of police officers. So naturally I am intrigued.'

Thin ice time again.

'I only told Darkman what I saw?' I said. 'And tell me, why did he come to you?'

'Darkman doesn't have the resources I have. He's been dipping too deep into his own sugar bowl. He's small-time rubbish. But he knows that Parker and I have been associates in the past. And also he knows that if I found out that he was aware of any information pertaining to Parker, or that Parker was in a position to be a threat to me, and Darkman hadn't told me, I'd skin him alive and nail his nigger hide to the nearest tree.'

Nice thought. 'As a matter of interest, what were you led to believe Parker had?' I asked. I was intrigued.

'I think I've exchanged quite enough information for now, Mr Sharman. You will be told more when and if I believe you need to know more.'

Fair enough, I thought, but I tried one more question. 'So what do you intend to do now?'

'I intend to liberate Parker and his money from the people he's with and make sure that he cannot harm me in the future.'

'Kill him, you mean.'

'Not necessarily. We had other plans for Mr Parker, but we will do what is necessary. Whatever it takes, Mr Sharman. And I also intend to keep you out of circulation for the foreseeable future.'

'Kill me?'

'I don't think so. At the moment you represent no threat to me or mine. But you could be useful to us, so look upon it as a holiday.'

'I already have plans for the holidays.'

'Cancel them. Or we'll cancel them for you. There's a room upstairs and we have a pretty good cook here. Soul food. I think you'll enjoy your stay.'

I didn't have much choice, so when Harold came back in, obviously summoned by Mr B.'s panic button again, I just drained my glass and followed him out of the room.

33

Friday night/Saturday morning

Harold took me upstairs to a room at the front of the house. It was medium-sized, warm, and contained a bed, wardrobe and dressing table. All I wanted right then.

'Toilet's opposite,' he said, tossing me my bag, which I could feel by the weight was sans ordnance. 'You need anything?'

'Just some sleep.'

'Do it. You want breakfast in bed and the papers?' He was kidding. Or maybe he wasn't.

'No thanks,' I replied. 'I'll come down early.'

'There's always someone round. Mr B. eats alone. The help eat in the kitchen at the back. Martha'll see to you.'

'Martha?'

'She's the cook, mon. Best in South London. You wait till you taste her chips.'

'OK, Harold,' I said. 'Thanks.'

'Don't thank me, mon. Thank all that money you seen.' And he left.

Jesus, I thought as I undressed and slipped between the sheets. What webs of lies we weave, and what trouble they eventually land us in.

But even so, I was asleep within minutes.

I woke just after seven by my watch and went to the bathroom to make my toilet. The house was peaceful and quiet and I got dressed and went downstairs. There were no armed guards on the front door, but it didn't even cross my mind to leave. Where would I go? I found the spotlessly clean kitchen by following my nose, and a big yellow woman was at the stove stirring a pot of something that made my mouth water. Jazz FM was on a small radio on the dresser. Cannonball Adderley.

She looked round as I entered. 'Hi,' she said. 'No one told me we had visitors.'

'I was a late arrival,' I said. 'You must be Martha.'

'That's my name, don't wear it out.' She seemed in good humour, and not the least fazed by my appearance. She must've been used to strangers.

'I'm Nick,' I said.

'Hi, Nick.'

'Hi, Martha. Something smells good.'

'Gumbo,' she said. 'For later. You want coffee?'

'Sure.'

'Sit down.'

I took a chair by the long, polished table that sat in the middle of the floor, and she rescued a pot off the stove and a mug from a shelf and stuck them both under my nose. 'Help yourself.'

I did and it tasted good.

'Breakfast?' she asked.

'Lead me to it.'

'Bacon, eggs, plantain, beans and chips?'

'Sounds like it's got my name on it.'

She shoved some bread in the toaster and went to the fridge to get the makings. When they were sizzling in various pans, I poured another coffee, lit a cigarette and said. 'Where is everybody?'

'Mr B. like to sleep late Sat'day. Harold and Marcus, they be sleeping too. Goldie's out back taking care of business.'

'Anybody else live here?'

'You're nosy.'

'Sorry. Force of habit. Are there?'

'Not right now. People come and go.' She started to slip food on to a plate and I dogged out my cigarette. She put toast on the side and pointed to the butter and condiments on the dresser.

I dug in. Harold was right. Her chips were great.

34

As I was finishing my food, the geezer with all the gold teeth came into the kitchen. He had to be Goldie. Hey, I'm a detective. I can work things out like that in a flash. In one hand he was carrying a rifle that he propped against the dresser, and in the other, a pile of newspapers that he dropped on the table, then made a pistol out of his right hand and pointed it at me. 'Breakfast, Goldie?' said Martha, which proved my powers of deduction were spot on, as usual.

'Sure, baby,' he replied, and sat down opposite me.

I picked up a copy of the *Telegraph* from the top of the pile and found a little bit about myself on page three. Still wanted. Well, it was nice to be popular for a change.

Goldie took a pack of Marlboro out of his sweatshirt pocket and offered them to me. 'How you doin', mon,' he said, with a flash of yellow metal in his smile.

'Not too bad,' and I took a cigarette and lit both his and mine with my Zippo.

'I hear we're all goin' visitin' this a.m.'

'Is that right? Anyone I know?'

'Don't know who you know, mon. But these are bad people. Lawless. Desperadoes. You know what I mean?'

My heart sank. 'I know,' I said.

'But we badder,' and he winked.

Martha served him up a huge plate of food and he dug in, and I went back to the papers. Someone was a big reader, because there was a copy of every single national newspaper, and I featured in most. The investigation of the murders at the hotel was ongoing and an early arrest was expected.

That was what I was afraid of.

Just as Goldie was wiping the last of his egg yolk from the plate with a crust of bread, Harold came into the kitchen. It was a regular café round here.

'Martha, honey,' he said, whirling her around the room. 'Get rattlin' them pots and pans. I'm a hungry man and there's work to do today.'

'You put me down!' she screeched, but I could tell she loved the attention. 'You boys'll be the death of me, and I got Mr B.'s breakfast to fix.'

'Well, do everything double and gimme a plate,' he said, letting her go and going to the fridge for some juice. 'Today we're gonna make our Christmas bonus,' and he gave me a big grin.

Or not, as the case may be, I thought.

35

Martha got busy at the stove again and made up two more plates of breakfast. One she put in front of Harold, who'd joined Goldie and me at the table, and the other she put on a prepared tray with a pot of coffee and the papers and left the room. When she came back empty-handed she said, 'Mr B. wants to see you lot and Marcus in an hour in his office.'

'No problem,' said Harold. 'But I'd better dig that Marcus out of his pit. Get some more coffee on, Martha, I think he had a kinda late night.' And he left the room too.

Marcus looked like shit when he came into the kitchen ten minutes later, wearing a T-shirt and mohair strides, and the look on his face when he spotted me gave me the impression he thought pretty much the same about my presence there. He rubbed his unruly hair and slumped at the table where Martha shoved a mug of coffee under his nose. 'Too damn early,' he said. 'I shoulda stayed with my woman last night.'

'Mr B. wouldn't like that,' said Harold, who'd come in close behind him. 'And you know how he get when he don't like things.'

'Sure, man,' said Marcus, pushing his beak into his mug and slurping up some of the hot liquid. 'I know how he get.'

'So be a good boy and button your lip,' Harold went on. 'You don't know when you're well off.'

Marcus grunted and scratched under one arm. 'I know,' he said.

Before we all presented ourselves at the ordained hour in Mr B.'s sanctum, I went up to my room and broke out the remains of my cocaine. I had a feeling I'd be in need of a livener before the day was out. I looked at myself in the mirror of the dressing table before I went back down, and shook my head at the reflection I saw. Shit, I thought. What the fuck am I turning into? And when will this all end?

When the four of us trooped in to see Mr B., the curtains in his room were still drawn, and the only light apart from the aquarium, where fishy eyes regarded us coldly, was a tiny lamp on one table. Mr B. was wearing a suit, white shirt and tie, and he'd put on his shades again against the glare.

'I trust you slept well, Mr Sharman?' he said.

'Like a log. I always sleep better when the cops are on my tail.'

'Don't worry about them. We have other fish to fry.' And I knew he wasn't referring to his finny friends behind the wall of glass. 'Do you know Tootsie Rollins?'

112

'Sounds like a kind of sweetie.'

'Anything but. Do you know him?'

I shrugged. 'Never heard of him.'

'Probably just as well. But you will. He is a gangster. A vicious man. It was his crew that killed the policemen at the hotel and it is he who has Parker.'

'Did Parker go of his own accord? Did he fall or was he pushed?' I asked.

'It hardly matters. Parker had something that Rollins wanted. Something we all want. Something that belongs to me. And the money too, according to you. It is all most inconvenient that it was waylaid before I could get it. Most inconvenient.'

'What did Rollins want?' I asked, before we could get on to the contentious subject of the non-existent money again.

'Drugs. Weight of cocaine that Parker had brought into this country.'

I suddenly got the plot. I'd invented a load of money, but in fact Parker *had* had something. A load of dope. What a dickhead I'd been. I should've guessed.

'But Parker was working with the police?' I said.

'Precisely. What better way of smuggling a load of merchandise into the country? Arriving with New York's finest, rushed through immigration and customs with no worries.'

'Shit,' I said. 'That's diabolical. If you set it to music you'd have a hit.'

36

'So where are we going?' I asked Mr B., pre-empting the others.

'You're going to see Tootsie Rollins,' he replied.

'So where does this geezer Rollins hang out?' I asked.

'He has a variety of addresses,' replied Mr B. 'A recording studio in Peckham, a house in Putney, another in Kennington, a flat in Brixton, and some other places dotted around. He likes to keep his options open. But they're all in south London. That's his area and he rarely ventures out of it.'

'I *am* surprised I've never heard of him, then. So where is he now? And where's Parker?'

'My informants tell me that Parker is staying at the house in Kennington under close guard.'

'For his protection or to keep him prisoner?'

'As I said before, that hardly matters. But to be honest, I don't know.'

'There's only one way to find out,' said Harold. 'Pay him a visit.'

'Hold on,' I said. 'How many guards?'

'Half a dozen,' said Mr B.

'And there's just four of us,' I said. 'Bad odds.'

'These are not my only troops,' said Mr B. 'I can call up an army within minutes.'

'Better get them then,' I said. 'Unless you want a bloodbath on your hands.'

'They're on their way,' and as if to confirm his statement, Martha knocked on the door, opened it and said. 'Some of the boys to see you, Mr B.'

'Harold,' said Mr B. 'You take charge. Call me on your mobile when you've seen Tootsie. I'll be waiting for your call.'

'No problem, Boss,' said Harold. 'Come on you lot, let's go.'

The four of us filed out into the hall and went to the foyer, leaving Mr B. to feed the fishes or do the *Guardian* crossword, or whatever he did to pass his time waiting for news from the front. Waiting for us were four more black geezers, all looking like extras from a bad episode of *The Bill*, all dreadlocks and silly hats. Mind you, as these dudes were for real, I suppose *The Bill* got it right.

They were all fiddling with a variety of weapons. Revolvers, semi-automatic Browning Hi-Powers, the weapon of choice in south London, or else sawn-off shotguns loaded for bear.

'I don't have a gun, Harold,' I said. 'And that's making me feel underdressed for the party.'

'No worries,' he replied, producing my Detonics from under his jacket and tossing it to me. 'Just make sure you point it in the right direction.'

I dropped the mag out of the butt, checked that it was fully loaded, slapped the clip back home and put one shell into the breech. 'Don't worry about me,' I said. 'I know what I'm doing.'

Harold laconically introduced me to the rest of the wild bunch, but didn't bother with their names. They gave me a whole load of dirty looks, and we went outside to where Marcus's BMW and a fairly new Audi saloon were parked at the kerb.

I got in the back of the Beemer with Goldie, Marcus took the wheel and Harold rode shotgun. The other four guys got into the Audi, and it followed us as we pulled away.

It was only a short run to Kennington and the milkman was

still rattling bottles on to doorsteps as we arrived at a fairly affluent-looking estate of new, yellow-brick houses close to the river.

'All out,' said Harold and we exited the car, then he gestured for the rest to leave the Audi and the eight of us stood in the chill, grey morning air and stamped our feet in the dirty snow that still carpeted the street.

'Let's take it easy now, boys,' said Harold. 'No point in blasting our way in when we can go in cool. It's Christmas in a few days and I'm sure we all want to be around to enjoy the festivities. So go in nice. But remember, if any fucker inside gets feisty, kill 'im.'

37

The posse started rattling on in patois, probably thinking I wouldn't understand. But black geezers have been doing that to me since I was fifteen, and once you pick up the rhythm, it's as easy as easy to understand. I won't try and mimic it, just translate for the uninitiated.

'Round the back, you two,' Harold said to a couple of the biggest geezers. 'And don't let anyone get out.' Harold was changing his style from the laid-back, stoned-out dude I'd met the previous night, and I was beginning to realize why Mr B. trusted him with the job of leading us.

'No problem,' replied one of them, an evil-looking fucker with a cast in his left eye and two big gold rings in his right ear. He loped off with his mate and they vanished into a walkway.

'Majesty,' Harold said to another of the blokes who'd turned up at the house. 'You watch the front and the cars. No one gets out that way either.'

Majesty, who was as tall and regal as his name, spat into the gutter, tapped the sawn-off that was concealed under his long, dark-green overcoat and said, 'Yo.' Obviously a man of few words, our Majesty. Good name though.

'The rest of you come with me,' said Harold. 'And remember, no shooting unless it's absolutely necessary. We don't know who the hell we're going to find in there.'

At his words, Goldie, Marcus, the other unnamed soldier and I followed Harold up the garden path.

Harold gave the door a serious rat-a-tat-tat with his fist and waited. There was no answer, so he did it again. All was silent inside. 'Chick,' he said to the other geezer who hadn't been introduced. 'Do the business.'

From under his leather coat, Chick pulled out a short sledgehammer and, when we were all standing out of the way, swung it hard at the woodwork of the door. Once, twice, three times he whacked it, until with a screech of breaking wood it collapsed inwards. There was 'WELCOME' written on the doormat inside.

We took it at its word and pushed through into what appeared to be an average suburban dwelling, and for a moment I thought we were in the wrong house, until a squat black geezer, naked to the waist and wearing just a pair of denims, appeared at the other end of the corridor, an Ingram Mach 10 machine pistol clenched in his hands.

'Whoa,' said Harold. 'Put the gun down, Ramon, you're outnumbered.'

Outnumbered he might've been, but the gun he was holding was loaded with a thirty-shot magazine and shooting

117

down the narrow hallway he would've been hard-pressed to miss.

Shit, I thought. It's over before it's begun.

38

I tensed myself for the hail of bullets from the gun, when the bloke with the bad eye appeared behind the squat geezer, stuck his Browning into his ear and said, 'Pull the trigger and you're one dead motherfucker.'

The squat geezer, Ramon, relaxed his hold on the Ingram and Bad Eye relieved him of the weapon, much to my, and probably everyone else's, relief.

Harold walked up to Ramon, popped him a good one in his eye and said, 'Where's Tootsie at?'

'Tootsie's up here,' said a voice from the dark at the top of the stairs. 'And Tootsie's not happy. You fucked my door, man. That door cost me plenty.'

Harold walked back to the foot of the flight and said, 'Mr B.'ll pay. Just put in an invoice. Now come down here, Tootsie, and join us. We gotta talk.'

I was beginning to wonder why none of the neighbours had called the Bill. Maybe Tootsie had unexpected visitors every Saturday morning. Or maybe they knew to keep a low profile and let the brothers work out their own problems.

Probably the latter.

Definitely the latter, I decided when I saw Tootsie lumber into view, using the banister for balance. The geezer must've weighed twenty-five stone if he weighed an ounce and most of it seemed to be round his belly and backside. And he was as ugly as a bucket of frogs.

He eased himself down the stairs and the hall suddenly seemed like it was packed to the gunwales. Tootsie said tetchily, 'Get in the living room. We can't talk out here.'

Pretty civilized behaviour really, under the circumstances. That is, if you discounted the Ingram.

We did as Tootsie said, dragging Ramon, who was going to have a hell of a shiner later, with us, and keeping our weapons handy. Who knew what might be waiting in the living room? An anti-tank gun, possibly.

But there was nothing like that. Just a three-piece suite in tan leather; a pink carpet; several paintings, that veered dangerously close to kitsch; a TV, video and stereo system with satellite attachments that hadn't left much change out of five grand, and a long dining table with half a dozen chairs. The magnolia silk curtains were drawn tight and Tootsie left them like that, putting on a standard lamp with a pale-blue tasselled shade as he passed. I wondered if Tootsie had trouble with his colour definition.

He lowered himself on to the sofa and regarded us through piggy eyes almost lost in the flesh of his face. 'So what the fuck's the meaning of this intrusion?' he demanded. 'Harold. You'd better have a good reason bursting in here and bringing grey meat with you, or I'll personally see your nappy head on a pole.'

Grey meat? Did he mean me?

39

'We hear you've got a visitor, Tootsie,' said Harold.

'What's that got to do with you?'

'We hear he's carrying gear big time. And our pale friend here tells us he's gotta loada dough too.'

Tootsie gave me the evil eye. 'Your pale friend is lying.'

'Did you kill those cops at the Intercontinental?' I interjected.

'No, man, you did,' said Tootsie. 'It's been on TV so's it must be right.'

I felt like shoving my Detonics up his snout and popping off a cap, but I just nodded my head and said. 'Nice.'

Tootsie grinned.

'Is he here?' asked Harold.

'Who?' asked Tootsie innocently.

'Don't fuck with me, fatso,' said Harold. 'You're holding no cards.'

'I'm holding Parker,' said Tootsie. 'And he ain't here. Search the place if you like.'

Harold turned to Goldie and Bad Eye. 'You two, give the drum a spin.'

Off they went.

'So where is he?' asked Harold.

'Find out,' replied Tootsie. 'I ain't gonna give you no help.'

'Let's just shoot the bastard,' I said. 'This is all beginning to piss me off.'

Tootsie gave me the evil eye again. 'And start a war,' he said. 'Mr B. wouldn't like that.'

Fuck Mr B., and you too, I thought, but said nothing.

'So was Parker carrying weight?' asked Harold. 'And dough?'

'Weight maybe, but cash no,' replied Tootsie. 'I told you, your pale friend's fucking with your mind. You start listening to these bastards, you'll turn white yourself.'

'What do you say?' Harold said to me.

'You don't believe this fat fuck, do you?' I said. 'He's the one who's lying.'

Stalemate.

Goldie and Bad Eye came back then and Goldie shook his head. 'No one in the place,' he said.

'Told you,' said Tootsie.

'You're carrying a bit of weight yourself, Toots,' I said. 'Look at those love handles. Why don't I get a knife out of the kitchen and slice some of that meat off. Maybe you'd tell us where he is then.'

'You ain't got the bottle,' said Tootsie. But I could tell he wasn't sure.

'Try me,' and I looked him dead in the eye. 'Just try me, you fat cunt. It'd be my pleasure.'

40

'That's something I'd like to see,' said Harold.

Tootsie just grinned. He thought he'd got all the aces. That grin was beginning to get me well pissed off, and I thought it was time to get the fat man to spill some beans, so I cocked the hammer of the Detonics and did exactly what I'd thought of doing a few minutes earlier. I walked over to Tootsie and put the barrel against one of the nostrils of his flat nose. 'You don't know who you're dealing with here, son,' I said, looking down at him. 'I think I'd better tell you all about myself.'

'You ain't gonna pull that trigger,' he said, rather nasally.

'Ain't I?' I asked. 'Listen, son. I used to be a copper. I used to stitch up black boys like you every day. It's a wonder we never met, or believe me you'd've done some time. But I never had a gun then. Now I have. And now I don't have to stick to judges' rules or PACE, or whatever they're calling it this week. You think I won't pull the trigger? Try me, son. And I'll teach you the real meaning of Christmas.'

'Hey, man. I never done nothin' to you.'

'Haven't you? Then who blew up that plane at O'Hare Airport last week?'

He looked bewildered. 'What?'

It was an off-the-wall question as far as he was concerned, and the rest didn't know what the hell I was going on about.

'You heard,' I replied. 'And I heard it was some of your mates.'

'What about it?' he seemed genuinely puzzled, as if he blew up plane-loads of people every day. But I knew he knew what I was talking about.

'Was it?' I said.

'It might've been.'

'Why'd they do it?'

'What's the problem? It was a warning to Parker. Just to let him know what's what.'

'And what is what?'

I could hear my voice rising, and my grip on the pistol was sweaty and it was bumping Tootsie's nose. Hard.

'What's it to you?'

'Tell me what is what, Tootsie,' I repeated.

'Careful,' said Harold from behind me.

'Shut up, you,' I said. 'This is between me and him. So *what* is *what* motherfucker?' I demanded.

'We knew he was on the passenger list,' said Tootsie, for the first time really beginning to grasp the magnitude of the situation, if not why I was asking. 'But not on the plane. We wanted to make sure he knew we could get to him if we wanted.'

'So he'd bring the drugs over here?'

'Correct.'

'Why didn't he just deliver the stuff in the States?'

'Because there was a big contract out on him and he was shit-scared the guys would rip him off and kill him anyway. He got in touch with Mr B., and promised him the dope in exchange for a safe haven here. It seemed like the best plan to him.'

'But he was going into witness protection over there.'

'Big deal. Do you know how many people in the programme get their new identities blown every year? Loads. Those coppers'll sell their own mothers for fifty dollars, let alone some bad guy who's rolled over on his own. And he knew my people would get to him sooner or later. He decided he'd rather take his chances over here. Europe's a big place and you can get lost easy and live cheap too. He stole that dope, man, and my people wanted it back.'

'For fuck's sake. This is insane! And you were prepared to kill four hundred innocent people to make your point?'

Tootsie shrugged and I nearly hit him. 'Not me, man,' he said. 'I never placed no bomb.'

'But you know who did. And that makes you culpable.'

He looked lost at that. Obviously culpable wasn't in his vocabulary.

'Do you know who was on that plane?' I asked after a moment.

Another shrug.

'My ex-wife,' I said. 'And her new husband and their son. He was just a toddler.'

'What do you care if she was your *ex*-wife?' said Tootsie and I lost it. I pulled the gun back from his nose, smacked the end of the barrel against his forehead and my finger tightened on the trigger. And suddenly I heard more metallic clicks as Harold, Goldie, Chick and Bad Eye all levelled their guns at me and prepared to shoot.

'Cool down fire,' said Harold. 'He's no good to us dead.'

41

'I can pull this trigger before you can shoot me,' I said as calmly as possible under the circumstances, but the air in the room was thick with tension.

'Sure you can,' said Harold, equally as calm. 'And go ahead if that'll make you happy. But we'll waste you, man, promise. The fat boy will keep. Won't you, Toots? There'll be plenty of time for you to sort him.'

Tootsie's face was grey and sweaty, and he kept trying to move his head away from the barrel of my gun. But I kept following him until the back of his head was hard up against the cushion of the chair he was sitting in.

'Won't you, Toots?' Harold repeated, and Tootsie nodded slightly. 'And don't you want to see Parker?' Harold said to me. 'Don't you owe him one too?'

124

''Course I do,' I said. 'But the other face can tell us where he is, so we don't need Fat Boy.' I was referring to Ramon, who was standing against the wall looking like he wished he was anywhere but here, what with all the guns pointing in different directions, and the fact that a stray bullet might end his squat little life. And of course if there *was* a lot of shooting, the chance that in the end, him being a witness and all, the bullet might not be so stray.

'Yeah, but you want to see what happens next, don't you?' said Harold. 'And you won't if you're brown bread.'

It was my turn to nod, and I let the hammer of the .45 down gently, pulled it away from Tootsie's forehead and slid it into my pocket. My shoulders were stiff with stress and I eased them.

'That's better,' said Harold. 'Now, Tootsie. Tell us where the *raas* Parker is hiding, or else I'll let me white friend here do what he wants to you.'

Tootsie looked up and I saw fear in his eyes and winked. 'Blood *claat* man,' he said. 'He's at the social club.'

I looked at Harold for enlightenment. 'Loughborough,' he said. 'An old supermarket that Tootsie liberated from the Co-op. You paying them any rent, Toots, my man?'

Tootsie shook his head and Harold laughed. 'The shop sent the bailiffs in a couple o' years ago and Tootsie sent them home tied to an old milk float. Laugh? Hey, me almost bought a round! Come on, boys. You too, Tootsie. Me dyin' to meet our American friend.'

42

We all trooped out of the house, Tootsie and Ramon, who we allowed to pull on a sweater, under the watchful eyes of Goldie, Bad Eye, Marcus, and Chick. We rounded up the rest of the troops and squeezed into the cars.

On the way to the BMW, Harold said to me, 'Sorry about your old lady, man. That's a tough break.'

'Yeah,' I agreed. 'Except she wasn't my old lady any more.'

'Things stick,' he said. 'People stick. I got a babymother lives over Hackney way. I always say I ain't never gonna see her no more, but I always find my way round there come Sunday morning.'

'That's good, Harold,' I said. 'Maybe one day you'll stay.'

'No way, man. Me like other skirt too much for that. But I'll always keep in touch. Now come on, move your *raas*. Time's hurrying by.'

I sat in front of the Beemer this time, with Harold, Tootsie and Goldie filling the back seat to more than capacity. 'You fuckin' fat motherfucker,' complained Goldie to Tootsie. 'I can hardly breathe here and you stink. Don't you ever wash, man?'

Tootsie said nothing. I sat for most of the journey halfway round on my seat giving him the snake eye. He didn't look happy.

We got to the old supermarket in Loughborough fast. It was part of a single block, under a row of maisonettes that looked as dilapidated as the shop itself and its neighbours, some of which had been the victims of fire attacks by the looks of it. All the units, including the old Co-op, still

126

identifiable by a lopsided sign, were metalled up, and the whole place looked deserted.

We stopped the cars about a hundred yards from the shop, which was surrounded by a raised walkway, and sat in the looming shadows of four beat-up, water-stained, broken-windowed tower blocks. The whole estate looked about ready for the demolition men to move in, but would probably stand for another fifty years, a proud monument to post-war urban planning and backhanders to the builders.

'Yo, Tootsie,' said Harold. 'We're gonna go in. Now we can do it the nice way or the nasty way. I reckon the nice way's favourite with no gunshots or body count. And besides, we don't want to spoil the local dolites' well-deserved Saturday-morning lie-in, do we?'

Tootsie snarled something unintelligible. He was getting his bottle back and I didn't like that, so I snarled something unintelligible too and tapped the pistol butt protruding from my coat pocket, and Tootsie shut up as he remembered the open bore of the barrel of the Detonics bouncing around on his forehead.

'So?' said Harold.

'Save your ammunition,' said Tootsie. 'I'll take you inside.'

43

'Who's inside?' asked Harold.

'Parker and one of my guys. His minder,' said Tootsie.

'Armed?' Harold again.

'Sure.'

'And we just walk in calm as you please?'

'I'll go in alone.'

'I don't think so,' said Harold.

Tootsie thought about it for a moment, his brow wrinkled. 'I'll call him on the car phone,' he said.

Harold pondered the idea for a second. 'OK,' he agreed. 'But no tricks, or you're history.'

'No tricks,' said Tootsie. 'I ain't stupid.'

'Don't be,' I interjected. 'Just remember I'm watching you.'

Tootsie said nothing in reply, just accepted the car phone from Marcus and punched in a number.

The phone in his hand rang for a long time. It was silent in the car and we could hear the buzz of the tone. Then a voice. 'Clarence?' said Tootsie. These guys had great names. 'Tootsie. I'm outside coming in. I'm not alone ... That doesn't matter ... Listen, motherfucker, I don't want any arguments, just chill ... Is Parker OK? ... Fine. Two minutes.' And he killed the phone. 'Let's go,' he said.

We got out of our car and the others got out of theirs, and we moved off in a group towards the block of shops, Tootsie taking a keyring out of the side pocket of his enormous trousers as he went.

He undid two locks and pushed open the heavy metal door,

and the rest of us, apart from Ramon, pointed our weapons at the darkness inside. Nothing.

'In you go, Tootsie,' said Harold. 'Anybody shoots, you get it first. Man, no bullets could get through you! And put on some lights. You do have lights, don't you?'

Tootsie scowled, but did as he was told, and fluorescent tubes popped into life in the ceiling of the corridor that stretched ahead of us.

Tootsie walked in front, Harold next, then me, followed by the rest in what order I don't know. 'Pinpoint your man,' said Harold. He was a good first lieutenant.

'Clarence,' yelled Tootsie. 'Show yourself, man. It's cool.'

'Who's with you, Mr Tootsie?' said a voice from back in the building.

'Just some visitors,' said Tootsie. 'No problems.'

Santa and his helpers, I thought.

A figure emerged from in front of us, a skinny spade carrying a sawn-off shotgun. Everywhere I went lately there seemed to be more guns than Woolwich Arsenal.

'Put up the gun, Clarence,' said Tootsie. 'These gentlemen just want a word with Mr Parker. Is he fit to receive visitors?'

'Sure is, Mr Tootsie,' said Clarence, who pointed the shotgun to the floor. 'I just made him some nice scrambled eggs and bacon for breakfast, and he's watching the fights on Sky.'

'Nice for him,' said Tootsie. 'So lead on, Clarence. Don't let's be keeping our guests in the hall.'

Clarence turned and pushed open another door and we all filed through it. Inside was another world totally. Although the outside of the building looked like a khazi, someone had spent big bucks on the interior, although it was a trifle plush for my taste. The designer had gone an abundance on leather, velvet and damask, so that the huge room we found ourselves in reminded me strongly of an amateur production of *The Arabian Nights*. Parker was sprawled across a massive zebra-skin sofa with a beer in one hand and a cigarette in the other, in front of a giant-screen TV showing highlights of the last Nigel Benn championship fight.

He looked up with hooded eyes as we trooped in, and when he saw me he said, 'Well hello, Mr Sharman, I wondered when we'd meet again.'

44

Harold ignored Parker. 'Goldie! Marcus!' he barked. 'Check the rest of this place out. We don't want any little surprises, like a machine-gun nest in the kitchen.'

Clutching their weapons, the duo did as he said. With every minute I was gaining more respect for young Harold, even though I still thought he was a big-time pain in the arse.

When the pair had gone, Harold sat Tootsie down on the zebra-skin sofa next to Parker. He sat Clarence and Ramon – who hadn't spoken a word since he was captured – on one of a similar size, but upholstered in the black orange and green colours of Ras Tafari; switched off the TV set, pulled up a leather recliner and perched on the edge, his gun in his hand. The rest of us found seats of our own and sat in silence.

A couple of minutes later Goldie and Marcus came back. 'Cool, boss,' said Goldie. He was eating a Jamaican patty that was such a bright orange I reckoned it would probably glow in the dark.

'Cool,' said Harold. 'So where's the stash?' he said to Parker.

'Wait a minute,' I interrupted. 'Me first.'

'You ain't in charge here,' said Harold.

'So? But there's things I need to know.'

'And there's things *I* need to know,' said Harold, tapping his pistol barrel impatiently on his knee. 'And we don't know how long we've got. We've been lucky so far. We've got into two locations without any shooting. Our luck's gonna change sooner or later. Any minute now a whole lot of geezers could come through that door.' He gestured at the exit to the hall. 'With guns blazing. We've managed to contain the situations up to now, but that don't mean we will for ever.'

'So let's take Parker and Tootsie with us,' I said. 'We'll go somewhere where we can chat for a while without interruption.'

Harold looked at me hard. 'Man, don't get hung up on what's happened in the past,' he said. 'You can't change any of that shit, whatever you do to them.'

'But I can feel better about the situation.'

'No, man. We don't take any hostages past this point. It gets too complicated. All we want is the dope and the cash you saw and we're out of here.'

'Cash,' said Parker, suddenly alert. 'What cash?'

Everyone looked at me. 'Listen guys,' I said. 'I've got a tiny confession to make.'

45

'What kind of confession?' said Harold, bringing the gun up in my direction. I could tell he was getting a bit shirty, and frankly, all things considered, I couldn't blame him.

'About the money I said I saw.'

'Said?'

'Yeah. Well, see, I was in a bit of a hole at the time. I needed some help. So I told Darkman . . .'

'*Said.* Fuckin' *said.* What is fuckin' *said*?' demanded Harold. 'You mean it don't exist?'

'Well, no. But there's the weight. That exists.'

'Mother*fucker*!' screamed Harold, losing it a trifle. 'Mother-fucker. You screwed us good.'

'No, man,' I said placatingly, looking at the barrel of the pistol he was holding as he waved it around. 'There's the dope. You'll get the dope. Won't he Parker?' My mouth was dry but I'd swear, if something good didn't happen soon, my boxers would be wet.

Parker shook his head in amazement. 'You guys,' he drawled. 'Amateur night or what?'

'Tell him about the dope, Parker,' I insisted.

'There's dope,' said the American. 'Unfortunately I don't have access to it at the moment. My large friend here and his associates have confiscated the merchandise, and I sit here awaiting my fate.'

'So they did kidnap you?' I said.

'Yes.'

'And you didn't have anything to do with killing those coppers at the hotel?'

'They were looking after me. Why would I want them dead? They were my lifeline. So I would be grateful if you would take me with you when you leave. I mean, check out the accommodation. And as for where I'm sleeping . . .'

I looked again around the room, and despite it all, it was funny. 'I thought these were pretty snazzy digs, Parker,' I said. 'Maybe a little bright for my taste . . .'

'Not without the drugs,' interrupted Harold, obviously not amused.

'Tootsie,' I said, trying desperately to retrieve something from the mess I'd got myself into. 'It's shit or get off the pot time. We need that dope.' I saw Harold's face. '*I* need that dope. Badly. Otherwise both me and Mr Parker look like we're in the mire hip-deep.'

Tootsie shrugged. 'Find it,' he said.

'Oh yeah,' I replied. 'Which means me and Parker get topped and you have a merry Christmas bloating out on fried chicken.'

'No merry Christmas for *that* motherfucker,' growled Harold.

'Mexican stand-off time, Tootsie,' I said. 'We die, you die. But produce the weight and we all enjoy the holly and the ivy.'

'I have wages to pay,' said Tootsie, like some kind of small businessman caught up in the Brixton Challenge.

'Fuck the wages,' I said. 'This ain't a sodding debating society, Fat Man. Harold's right. We don't have much time, so cough the gear or cough your last breath.'

Melodramatic, but efficient.

'This means war,' said Tootsie to Harold. 'Mr B. better know that.'

133

'Mr B. ain't afraid of no blimp,' said Harold. 'He can take care of his own backyard.'

Tootsie shrugged. 'OK, but my American associates ain't gonna be best pleased if you take Parker.'

'Mr B. got American associates too,' said Harold scornfully. 'Maybe he do a deal with them for the dude.'

That didn't please Parker. 'You got my pension scheme, boy,' he said to Harold. 'What more do you want?'

Harold didn't reply, just said to Tootsie, 'Come on then, man, give up the stuff.'

Tootsie levered himself up from the seat. 'It's upstairs,' he said.

'Me and Sharman'll come with you,' said Harold. 'The rest of you truss up Tootsie's boys tight. We don't need nobody else to know what's happened here till we safe home. Come on, you,' he said to me. 'We ain't finished with your ass yet by a long way.'

I was afraid of that, but at least the trip hadn't been a total waste, so I followed Harold as he pushed Tootsie in front of him out into the corridor. We turned left and came to a double flight of stairs leading upwards. The stairs were lit from where Goldie and Marcus had made their recce and led into another corridor with doors off to both sides. Probably the old offices of the Co-op I thought, and was right.

The doors were all open and some had been converted into bedrooms, although nothing like as opulently as the room downstairs, and I saw what Parker meant about his sleeping accommodation.

The last door led into a room barely furnished with a desk and two chairs. Tootsie went to a wall cupboard and opened it. Inside was the face of a grey steel safe. Tootsie manipulated the combination and pulled open the heavy door. Inside that was a suitcase. Harold gestured for me to keep Tootsie covered, humped the case on to the desk and opened it. Inside were packets and packets of white powder. Weight, big time, as promised. Maybe a quarter of a million wholesale. Christ knows how much street value, after a few of the chaps had walked on it.

Harold grinned, Tootsie scowled, and I made no expression. Except deep inside I was mucho relieved. With all the dope about, maybe the boys would forget my previous misdemeanours.

'Good, Toots,' said Harold. 'You getting wise in your old age. Now we all go downstairs and we go home. A good morning's work.'

'You'll be sorry for this,' said Tootsie.

'Maybe, man,' said Harold.

'Definitely, man,' replied Tootsie. 'You and Sharman and Mr B. All of you. Take my word.'

'I doubt it,' said Harold.

He was going to live to regret those words.

46

After that, we all went back downstairs where Ramon and Clarence were tied back to back on the zebra-skin sofa. 'I want Tootsie,' I said to Harold.

'What for?' he asked.

'To take him to the cop shop and get me out of this mess.'

'No way,' said Harold. 'No Babylon. That ain't the way we operate. You'll have to sort that one out for yourself. We ain't here to fight your battles, just liberate the cocaine for the people of free Brixton. Thems that can afford it, of course,' he added with a grin.

'Harold,' I said as calmly as possible. 'I'm still wanted for murder. I need him.'

'Get him then. But get him in your own time.'

'But if I take him to the police it'll keep him off the streets and solve all our problems.'

'Not yours,' said Harold. 'We gotta tell Mr B. about the little porkies you told about the money first. He ain't gonna be well pleased.'

'He's got the dope, hasn't he?' I replied. 'What does he want? The world?'

'Yeah,' said Harold.

'But where would he put it?' I asked.

This was all getting a little too existential for Harold, who just scowled and shook his head. 'Don't get too clever, mon,' he said. 'Just 'cos we've had a result. Your troubles are just starting.'

Which about summed up all he knew about my troubles. 'And what about Parker?' I said, changing the subject. He hadn't been tied and was now sitting in the recliner puffing uneasily on another cigarette.

'Yeah. What about him?' mused Harold.

'Yes. What about me?' asked Parker.

'Parker comes with us,' said Harold. 'Mr B. wants to see him. He got plans for the man.'

'And we just leave Tootsie here?' I said.

'That's right,' said Harold. 'Truss up the fat turkey,' he ordered Goldie and Marcus. 'And be quick. I wanna get out of this dump pronto.'

I looked long and hard at the big black man. 'I'll be back,

son,' I promised. 'Soon. Tick-tock, motherfucker. Count the minutes, and keep looking over your shoulder, because pretty soon I'll be there.'

'Shut up, Sharman,' said Harold. 'Come on, you guys, get him tied up, this place gives me the creeps.'

Goldie and Marcus did as they were told, and within five minutes we were all back in our cars, complete with the cocaine and Parker. And not a shot had been fired.

But of course, I should've known that wouldn't last.

47

We were back at the house in Brixton in time for elevenses, which Martha served to the boys in the kitchen whilst Harold and I took Parker and the drugs in to see Mr B. I wasn't offered any tea and biscuits, which was just as well, as I had a feeling that I might throw up if I was. I was in deep trouble about the lies I'd told, and I wondered how Mr B. was going to react.

Harold hoisted the case on to the desk and opened it with a flourish. 'Weight, an' heavy,' he said proudly, as if he'd picked the leaves, processed the paste and dried it to powder personally.

'Cut us a line,' said Mr B. 'I always like to test the merchandise before giving a verdict.'

That was a tradition I most heartily endorsed.

Harold did the business with a Swiss Army knife that had more blades than a guards' officers' reunion, split a baggie, laid out more than a fair portion and chopped it into a dozen lines. Mr B. took out a brand-new fifty, rolled it up tight and had first dibs. He sat back in his chair with a grunt of satisfaction and gave the note to Harold who hoovered up a line, coughed and laughed. I got third hit and felt all the better for it. 'Parker?' I said to Mr B. when I was satisfied.

'Might as well,' said the big man, and I passed the fifty to our transatlantic visitor.

'Here goes nothing,' he said, and scarfed up his fair share.

We all sat back around Mr B.'s desk and looked at each other through the gloom. 'Good stuff,' said the boss to Parker. 'Why didn't you bring it to me first?'

'I had the cops up to my ass,' said the American. 'Then Tootsie killed them, and hijacked me and the stuff. He had a gang of cut-throats toting heavy-duty ordnance running round the place. What the hell was I supposed to do?'

'OK, Jefferson,' said Mr B. 'At least you're here now. But what was all this money I kept hearing about from Sharman?' And he fixed me with a gaze which I could see even through his Ray-Bans.

'I think Mr Sharman was running scared and concocted a story to keep him up with the action,' said Parker.

Very well put, I thought. I couldn't've précised the story better myself.

'Running scared, huh,' said Mr B. 'Is that about it?'

I nodded, then said, 'That's about it,' in case he hadn't seen my head move.

'You've got some nerve, Sharman, I'll give you that,' said Mr B. 'But I guess all's well that ends well.'

'But it hasn't ended yet,' I said, and even I didn't know how prophetic I was being.

48

'Meaning?' said Mr B.

'Meaning I'm still in the shit with the cops,' I replied.

'They aren't all you're in the shit with,' said Mr B. 'You're in the shit with me too, lying about the money and all.'

'It was all I could think of to stir things up. And it all worked out well enough in the end.'

'That's true,' he said. 'But I don't like being lied to.'

'Who does?' I said. 'But it happens to me all the time.'

'Tough,' said Mr B.

'So what do we do now?' I asked.

'*We* carry on with our lives,' said Mr B. 'You, on the other hand, are in a difficult position.'

'You can say that again.'

'Harold,' he said. 'Go round up the boys.'

The firing squad.

Harold stood up and left the room, and as the door clicked to behind him, I realized I was still armed.

Big mistake all round.

Parker wasn't armed. Mr B. might be. But more likely he had a weapon in the drawer of his desk. Why bother to pack heavy metal when he was surrounded by armed men? He was the boss, after all. There were some perks. And handguns tend to spoil the line of your suit.

I smiled to myself and hauled the Detonics from the waistband at the back of my trousers. There was still a bullet in the breech. I cocked the weapon. 'Sorry,' I said. 'But I think it's time for me to go.'

'Shit,' said Mr B., just loud enough for me to hear.

I stood, slammed the lid of the case closed and slipped the locks with my free hand. 'Just in case I need a bargaining tool later,' I said as I went, and drew the curtains back behind him. I'd been right. French windows let in the grey day from outside. I saw Mr B. wince and the scars on his face were livid in the thin light. I snapped the locks on the French windows and opened them. I looked back at the illuminated aquaria. 'If this was a film I'd blow that lot to hell and gone,' I said. 'But they've done nothing to me. See you later.' And I stepped outside on to the flagged patio, across a flower bed, on to the lawn and headed for the fence at the back that stood crookedly between two skeletal trees.

I heard no sign of pursuit from behind me.

I threw the bag over the fence and pulled myself up and over, after it. At the back was a narrow, overgrown path between the gardens. I picked up the case, turned left and ran along it. There was a T-junction at the end. I took another left and came to a solid-looking wooden door. I turned the handle and it opened. I let it slam behind me. There was no handle on the outside and I was in a parallel street to where the house was. On the corner I saw a red bus cross the junction and I headed that way and on to the main road. There was another bus just stopping opposite, heading towards the West End. I ran across the street, found some coins and joined the queue.

49

Saturday afternoon

When the bus got to Piccadilly Circus I jumped off at the lights and got lost in the crowds of last-minute Christmas shoppers.

I walked up Shaftesbury Avenue, turned into Soho and found a pub that wasn't too crowded, bought a pint and went to a table facing the door. I stayed there for an hour or more, thinking that everyone who clocked me was going to ring three nines, until I got just too paranoid and left. I spent the rest of the short winter's day in the Empire Leicester Square, watching the new Keanu Reeves movie about drug-dealers getting their comeuppance. It wasn't that good, but it was bright and noisy and passed the time well enough. Halfway through it, I took the case to the gents', sat on the closed toilet-seat lid in one of the stalls and had a good sample of the merchandise. When I went back to my seat the film looked better.

Around six, I went into the bustling London Saturday night and walked through to Holborn. It was cold and I was strung out. In Lincoln's Inn Fields I found a phone box that worked and called ex-DI Jack Robber at his sister's place in Worthing. I remembered the number but not the code, and had to ring directory enquiries. As I punched in the numbers I hoped that he would answer, and not his dragon of a sister. She had never liked me much, but after a little bit of business we'd got involved in left him in hospital with three bullet holes in sensitive parts of his anatomy, she had liked me even less. I'd tried to compensate for the injuries with over thirty thousand quid that I'd managed to salvage from the wreckage, and I hoped that he'd forgiven me. He was my last hope, and if he hadn't I was well and truly fucked.

He answered on the fourth ring. 'Robber,' I said when I recognized his voice. 'It's Nick Sharman.'

'I wondered when you'd call,' he said back. 'You've been on telly more than Barrymore these last few days.'

'Yeah, I know. I've been set up.'

'*No.*' His voice was loaded with sarcasm.

'Don't fuck about, Jack,' I said. 'It's the truth.'

'I wonder how many times I heard that particular statement during my long and illustrious career.'

'It's true.'

''Course it is.'

'And I need your help. There's no one else.'

'Remember what happened last time?'

'Jack. Last time you came to me. Remember? Because of money.'

'I remember.'

'And I weighed you in.'

'I remember that too.'

'Good. Now I need your help. Do you give it or not?'

'What's in it for me?'

Typical. 'I've got some gear,' I said. 'A lot. Liberated from the bad guys. But I thought you might help for old time's sake. Know what I mean?'

'All right. All right. Let me think. Where are you?'

'London. In town. Holborn.'

'Are you mobile?'

'No.'

'Can you get down to Norwood?'

142

'Yeah.'

'Remember my little widow woman? The one with the boarding house in Knights Hill?'

'Yeah.'

'Get down there. I'll warn her you're on your way.'

'Will she be all right?'

''Course. She knows how to keep her mouth shut. And it's Christmas. With a bit of luck the place should be empty. Get down there now. I'll ring you later.'

'You're not setting me up are you, Jack?'

''Course not.'

'I hope not, Jack.'

'Trust me. Get down there. I'll be along later. And I'll bring some wheels.' And he hung up in my ear.

50

Saturday evening

Maybe I was being overcautious and over-paranoid, but I decided to take a circuitous route to Norwood. And, as it turned out, it was a big mistake, like a lot of my ideas were. I should've just got a cab all the way, but I don't trust cabbies. They talk too much, and they always seem to watch *Crimestoppers*, *Crime Monthly* and *Crimewatch* and want to get in on the act. So I got the taxi I'd hailed in Holborn to drop me on the Albert Embankment, just before Vauxhall Cross. There's a tunnel under the railway arches there, close to the station, and on the other side a bus stop where I could get a bus that would drop me at Norwood Garage, which was just a cough and a spit from where Robber's widow had her boarding house.

I paid the cab and watched as it got lost in the traffic before I went into the tunnel that stank of old piss and was littered with the detritus of city life. The place was lit with fluorescent tubes, but some had died and never been replaced. I walked along the deserted tunnel, ducking in and out of the shadows, trying to keep as low a profile as possible, when a voice came from one of the deep niches that interrupted the brickwork every few yards and often housed homeless people wrapped in raggedy blankets. 'Got a spare ciggy, mate?'

I nearly jumped out of my skin as a figure emerged from the darkness. It belonged to a young geezer with long blond hair, wearing a nylon bomber jacket over blue jeans. 'Don't do that,' I said.

'I didn't mean to frighten you,' he said with a sarcastic grin.

'You didn't,' I replied. 'I was miles away.'

'Got a ciggy, then?'

'No,' I said. 'I don't smoke.'

Fuck his luck. Let him buy his own cigarettes. I buy mine.

'Got any change then?'

'No. Sorry.'

'You ain't sorry, man,' and he was joined by a black guy in a leather coat and baggy pants.

'Look,' I said, holding up my free hand in a gesture of surrender. 'I've got no cigarettes or change.'

'What's in the case?' said the blond.

'Just clothes,' I lied. 'I'm going away for Christmas.' Maybe it wasn't such a lie. If Old Bill caught up with me, I'd be going away for a lot of Christmases.

'Show,' said the blond.

'I don't think so,' I said. 'Now I've got a train to catch and I'm in a hurry.'

'Everyone's in a hurry,' said a third voice, and someone came from behind me to block my escape. Another white guy. Short dark hair this time, a thick sweater and dirty white trousers. 'No one has any time for anyone.'

'That man's got good time,' said the black guy. 'Check his watch.'

Instinctively I looked at my Rolex. A nice one. A present long ago. A day-date chronometer with a blue face in a solid 18-carat case with a gold bracelet. Too good to wear really. But what should I do? Put it in the bank?

'I'd like a watch like that,' said the black guy. 'Look good on me.' Black guys always like Rolexes. They're like BMWs they can wear on their wrists. But he wasn't having mine. No way.

I decided that discretion was the better part of valour. 'No, guys,' I said in a placatory tone. 'It's snide. Twenty-five quid from a bloke outside Selfridges. It makes my wrist go green. It's rubbish.'

'So give it up,' said Dark Hair, and produced a knife from his back pocket. 'And the case.'

'Yeah, give it up,' said Blondie and produced a blade of his own.

'Yeah, give it up, man,' said the black guy, and let a two-foot-long machete drop down neatly from his sleeve into his fist. I bet he practised in front of his bedroom mirror. 'Or I'll cut off your hand.'

And I could tell he was fucking serious. They all were. They were prepared to kill me for my watch.

'But if you did that,' I said, 'I'd go into shock and maybe die. If I didn't die from loss of blood first.'

The black geezer nodded. Bastard. I was beginning to get angry.

'All right,' I said calmly, put the case on the ground, reached over with my right hand, flicked the catch on the Rolex's bracelet, let the watch slide off my left wrist and into my hand where I held it up on my index finger. 'Let's get this straight. You'd be prepared to murder me for this?'

I just wanted to hear it.

'Sure, man,' said the black guy. 'That watch worth dough.'

'I told you it's snide.'

'We don't believe you,' said Dark Hair.

'But you'd kill me anyway?'

Three nods.

'But the big question is: would you be prepared to die for it?'

They all looked at each other.

'You see,' I explained, playing for time and hoping someone else would walk into the tunnel and interrupt, 'if you're prepared to kill for it, it stands to reason you have to be prepared to die for it too.'

'Bollocks,' said Blondie.

'Because I'm carrying.' I went on as if he hadn't spoken.

'Sure,' said Blondie. 'Sure you are.'

I put my hand inside my coat and felt the butt of the Detonics. 'The next question is: are you prepared to stake your lives on it?'

'We're wasting time,' said the black guy. 'That's the oldest trick in the book,' and he raised the machete.

'There's always got to be one, hasn't there?' I said. 'One stupid bastard who won't take no for an answer. One stupid bastard who has to try and spoil it for everyone. And, son, today, you're that one stupid bastard.'

'Fuck you,' he said.

So I pulled out the Detonics and shot him straight between the eyes. The sound of the shot was loud in the silence of the tunnel and echoed for what seemed like for ever, and a thousand pigeons that were roosting in the roof took off with a beating of wings and a shower of dirt from their nests.

The black geezer dropped the machete with a clatter and went down hard. Then I gut-shot Dark Hair. He dropped his knife too, and sat down with a look of amazement in his eyes.

Blondie turned to run. 'Wait,' I said through the ringing in my ears.

'Don't shoot me, mister,' he begged as he turned back slowly. 'It was them.'

'I don't think so,' I said.

'Honest! They made me do it.'

'But you've seen me,' I said. 'And that's very bad news for both of us. Come here.'

'Don't hurt—'

'Save it,' I said. 'Close your eyes and open your mouth.'

He didn't do either, so I forced the muzzle of the gun into his mouth, breaking teeth as it went. He went down on his knees and reached up to me. I pulled the trigger and blew the back of his head off. Then I finished off Dark Hair with a shot to the back of his neck, left them and their weapons where they lay, put my watch back on, picked up the case and went for a drink.

It's thirsty work protecting your assets.

147

51

Saturday night

I got to the boarding house around eight-thirty. I was as jittery as a barrow of monkeys, half pissed and stoned to the bone by then. I wished I'd handled those kids better, but it was too late for regrets. Just put it down to experience and wear a cheap Timex in future. If indeed there was a future for me.

A low, freezing mist had come down across south London, and the street lights were just balls of yellow that did nothing to illuminate the darkness as I walked the few hundred yards from where I was dropped by the bus I'd caught outside the pub, more than a mile away from the killing ground. And when I knocked on the widow's door, my clothes and hair were dotted with drops of moisture and my breath plumed from my mouth like steam.

She answered within a moment, looked up and down the deserted street and hustled me inside. She was as plump and blonde as I remembered. 'Were you followed?' she asked.

'No,' I said. 'I'm all alone. I wouldn't have come here if I thought I'd got company.'

'I don't know why I'm doing this,' she said. 'I must be mad. Jack said he'd be here about ten. The fog's much worse on the coast.'

She led me into her comfortable, warm little living room where the TV was chattering to itself in the corner. 'Have you eaten?' she said.

I hadn't, and I thought I'd have no appetite after what had happened earlier, but suddenly I was starving. 'No,' I said.

'Egg and bacon?'

'Please.' And she bustled off to the kitchen.

'Tea?' she said, sticking her head back round the door. 'Or something stronger?'

'Both please,' I said. 'Is anyone else here?'

'Just the top back,' she replied. 'But you never see him. The others have gone away for the holidays. I'll put you in the middle front. Jack can come in with me.' And she blushed slightly.

Lucky Jack, I thought.

We watched the nine o'clock news as I ate my food, and drank the tea and large Scotch she'd brought me. I wasn't featured, which was good, but there was a late-breaking story about a triple shooting in Vauxhall. Drugs and gangs were mentioned. I said nothing.

The widow and I were watching the late film when we heard the whine of a car's transmission outside and the slamming of a door. I peered through the curtains and watched Robber walk away from an antique Morris 1000 Traveller with real wood panels.

Welcome to the nineties, Jack, I thought as the widow went to let him in.

52

The widow went to the front door and Robber came into the living room wiping moisture off his face. 'It's fucking murder out there,' he said grumpily. 'I was nearly killed three times driving up.'

I stood up and offered my hand. 'And a very good evening to you too, Jack,' I said.

He ignored my mitten, dropped the overnight bag that was hanging from his shoulder and shrugged out of his coat.

I kept my hand outstretched. 'Jack,' I said, nodding down in its direction.

He scowled, but took it anyway and gave it a perfunctory shake. 'That's better,' I said. 'I see you're in one of your usual sunny moods.'

'Bollocks,' he growled.

'Something to drink, Jack?' asked the widow, to break the silence that followed.

'I thought you'd never ask. Scotch.'

'Please,' she said.

'Please,' he added, then almost cracked a smile and said. 'Sorry. But those roads.'

'I understand,' she said, bobbed up and kissed him on the cheek and left the room.

Robber fell into an armchair and I took the sofa. 'Thanks for coming,' I said.

'You need bloody someone to look after you.'

'You're right. And I appreciate it.'

'So what happened?'

I drew a breath as the widow came back with fresh glasses

and the bottle, and over the next half-hour I told them both the whole story. Only leaving out my recent contretemps in Vauxhall. I didn't think they really needed to know about that.

When I'd finished, Robber shook his head. 'Christ,' he said. 'How do you manage it?'

'God knows,' I replied. 'Just lucky, I guess.'

'And you want my help?'

'That's why I phoned.'

'I don't know what to say Sharman,' he said. 'Every time I help you I seem to end up in hospital.'

'It's only happened once.'

'So far,' he said and lapsed into a sullen silence.

53

'Nellie,' he said to the widow after a moment or two. 'You go on up. I need to talk to Nick on his own.'

'Will you be long?' she asked. I think Nellie fancied a spot of rumpy-pumpy as a Christmas bonus.

'No,' he replied.

'Then I'll say goodnight,' she said. 'You know where you are, Mr Sharman. The room above this one. I've put clean sheets on the bed, and the central heating's on.'

'Thanks,' I said. 'I'll find it.'

She left us then and Robber poured two more glasses of Scotch. 'All right, Sharman,' he said. 'What've you got?'

I nodded at the case and he hauled it up on to his lap and opened it. He whistled when he saw the contents. 'How much?' he asked.

'About quarter of a million wholesale. Christ knows how much on the street.'

'I see you've given it a field test. Any good?'

'Very.'

'Well that's something. You armed?'

I showed him the Detonics. 'I've only got a couple of rounds, though,' I said. 'And I had to leave a couple more guns round Mr B.'s gaff. How about you?'

'I can't afford not to be with you around,' he replied, dumped the case on the coffee table, picked up the bag he'd brought, unzipped the top and brought out a brushed silver S&W .44 magnum.

'Dirty Harry,' I said. 'What do you use that for down in Worthing? Shooting rabbits?'

'If I did with a gun this size they'd be minced and cooked before they hit the ground.'

'Bunnyburgers,' I said with a grin. 'Christ, Jack. but it's good to see you.'

54

'I wish I was sure I could say the same for you,' he said, but I could tell he was pleased. As pleased as Robber was ever likely to get, anyhow.

'And what's with that bloody old car?' I said. 'What will it do? Nought to sixty in three weeks?'

'You got anything better?' said Robber. 'It's my sister's motor. Mine's in the garage with a duff gearbox. And it looks like I won't get it back till the new year. It pisses me off. I spend nearly twenty grand on a previously owned M-reg Mercedes and the sodding thing's always playing me up.'

'That's German efficiency for you,' I remarked. 'But at least you've got a good old Cowley machine to keep us out of trouble. Now tell me. Do you know these Mr B. and Tootsie characters?'

'I'm surprised *you* don't. Lee Byron, a.k.a. The Reverend Mr Black or Mr B. He ran an evangelical church in Dalston as a front for drug peddling. He got chased out of there on the hurry-up about ten years ago. But he'd made a packet and bought that house in Brixton, reconverted it from flats and spent a fortune on antique furniture. He stays there with a posse of bad black boys. He's got Yardie affiliates all over the world.'

'And he's still there.'

'What do you mean?'

'Why hasn't he been nicked, if everyone knows his game?'

'Use your bloody loaf, Sharman. What do you think? He keeps the wheels oiled, of course. Besides, if every guilty sod in this part of the world was where he should be, we'd need another hundred prisons the size of Parkhurst. And where would Lambeth get council tax? The streets would be bloody empty.'

'And Tootsie?' I asked, ignoring his diatribe.

'Failed reggae producer and promoter turned *gangsta*. He listened to all those rap records about killing the police and took it literally. He's a nasty little bastard. Or big bastard, I should say. We had him down for killing that poor bloody unarmed PC in Herne Hill two years ago. But we couldn't make it stick.'

'He killed Laura and her family,' I said. 'Or at least his pals in the States did.'

'You're sure?'

'He admitted it. I already told you that.'

'I'm sorry about Laura. And her husband and the kid.'

'And the rest of the poor bastards on the plane.'

He nodded.

'Then there's Parker and the Darkman,' I said.

'Parker I've never heard of. But that's not surprising as he's a Yank. But isn't Darkman an old mate of yours?'

'I didn't exactly have him round for dinner on a regular basis, but I know him.'

'I just bet you do.'

'But he's gone even stranger than he was before. Crack.'

Another nod from Robber.

'All in all a lovely collection,' I said.

'The world would be a better place without them, I'll say that.'

'And the world might have to get along without me if they catch up with me,' I said. 'That's why I want to catch up with them first, if that's possible. Judith could've been on that sodding plane with Laura.'

'You're going to have to prove it.'

'Not necessarily.'

'Meaning?'

'Meaning that there's more than one way to skin a cat, or a bunch of cats for that matter. The proper way. The proof way could take years. Or never happen. And meanwhile I'm banged up for murder and the judge has got his black cap on. Maybe I'll never be able to find out who actually planted the bomb. Maybe no one will. But there's a bunch of characters right here who were all webbed up in it. And Tootsie and his mob did kill those people at the hotel. That's for sure. If we can bring him down and as many of his friends and enemies as possible, at least I'll have that satisfaction. And I'll be in the clear. Otherwise I remain Britain's most wanted. You in?'

He thought about it for a minute. 'Any more where that came from?' he asked, nodding at the case.

I hesitated. I didn't know. But I needed Jack Robber and his car and blunderbuss, so without any more thought I told a porky pie again. ''Course,' I said. 'Tons. Enough for half a dozen brand new Mercedes and a country house thrown in.'

55

He thought about it for a minute, then grimaced. 'Yeah,' he said. 'I'm in.'

'Good,' I said. 'Let's drink to it.'

He poured me another glass, and we sat in silence for a while. 'Do you sometimes wonder if we've wandered into hell, Jack?' I asked eventually.

'Here we go,' he said.

'Seriously, do you?' I pressed.

'Sometimes. But if this is hell, why do we carry on thinking we might go there when we die?'

'Because there's always someone worse off, and that would be the *real* hell.'

'Sure.'

'What do you reckon the real hell's like then Jack?' I asked.

'No fags. No booze. No saturated fats or pork pies.'

'Sounds like your sister's house down in Worthing.'

'It bloody is, too.'

He cogitated for a moment as he drank his Scotch and lit a Benson's. 'What about you, Nick?'

'Having to watch Riverdance all day on TV.'

'Is that it?'

'And the shopping channels.'

'There's some nice birds in that Riverdance,' he said.

'Yeah, but it's still the most boring thing I've ever seen.'

'Nice legs,' he went on. 'Short skirts. Do you think you could see what colour knickers they're wearing from the front row?'

'Fancy booking a matinée to find out?' I said. 'But no ticket for me, thanks.'

'Or even if they've got knickers on at all,' he mused.

'They might forget.'

'They might.'

'But not if you went, Jack. Sod's law.'

'My sister watches the shopping channels,' he said.

'*You've* got a satellite, Jack?'

'Cable. A satellite would've spoiled the house value. Marge said that.' Marge was his sister.

'And you watch the shopping channels?'

'Sport mostly.'

'But Marge likes to spot a bargain.'

'Too bloody right. Have you ever seen them?'

'Now and again.'

'Horrible jewellery with fake stones. Lots of cleaning materials. Have you noticed that?'

'Not really.'

'Marge likes the cleaning materials. And slimming aids. There's a lot of those, too – pity she doesn't go in for those particular items. And she likes models of the Starship Enterprise. And old American cars.'

'Real old American cars?'

'No. Little models. Well, not so little, really.' He held his hands about a foot apart. 'This big.'

'So does Marge buy a lot?'

He looked to see if I was taking the piss. 'You taking the piss?' he asked.

'No. I'm interested.'

'Blimey, Nick, if you only knew.'

'Well tell me!'

'A tin tray with a picture of Elvis on it.'

'Early or late?'

'The Las Vegas years.'

'Cool. Is that all?'

'No. Not at all. Cleaning materials, like I told you. There's so much in the garage we can't get the bloody car in. And models of little houses. To make up a village. A pub, the village shop and all the people. She keeps them on the sideboard. I swear she talks to them. "Hello, Mr Brown the baker. Good morning, Constable Smith." I think she's going mad. I had to get away. That's why I was glad you phoned.'

'Nothing to do with my predicament?'

'And that too.'

'And a chance to see the buxom widow.'

'And that too.'

'So, Jack. Apart from Riverdance, you've pretty well got hell sewn up on the south coast.'

'Pretty well.'

'Well, it seems to me I've got it sorted out up here. So welcome to my version of hell.'

'It could be worse.'

'I don't think so.'

But of course I was wrong.

56

After that, we sat talking until the Scotch bottle was empty, trying to come up with a plan, but with little success. There were only two of us, and loads of them. Who knew how many if the word went out? And we had just two guns and a few bullets between us, whilst they had an armoury. 'It's going to be tough,' said Robber in a serious understatement. 'Very tough.'

'We know that,' I said. 'But what are we going to do?'

'Christ knows. Vamp it.'

'As per bloody usual. I'm getting tired of having to vamp it every time I do a job.'

'They're the kind of jobs you get.'

'Tell me about it.'

'How's Judith?' he asked after a moment, changing the subject.

'Shit,' I said. 'I should've been in touch.' I looked at the widow's phone, but I couldn't use it. It was insecure. Too many ways of getting the number these days, and I cursed at having thrown away Latimer's portable phone. 'You still got a mobile?' I asked.

Robber nodded.

'Give us it, I'll call her up.'

'Bit late, isn't it?'

'She'll be up. She's a night bird.'

He pulled a Nokia mobile out of his pocket, switched it on and passed it over. I punched in Jane's number and looked at my Rolex and felt a stab of guilt about the three lives I'd stopped in Vauxhall. And now I was getting on my high horse about some other murderers. Still, that's life. No one ever said it was going to be perfect. It was nearly midnight and I bet myself Judith was watching some post-pub entertainment on Channel 4 featuring well-fit young people getting their kit off.

She answered on the third ring. 'Judith Sharman,' she said.

'I knew you'd be up.'

'Dad! Thank goodness. I've been frantic.'

I could hear voices in the background. And music. And laughter. Electronic stylee. 'Are you alone?' I asked.

'Yes. They've gone to bed.'

'What are you watching?'

'Some silly programme.'

'*The Girlie Show?*'

'Something like that. Where are you?'

'I can't tell you. You never know who's listening. But I'm all right.'

'You're still in trouble. The police were round again today.'

'I know. But it's going to be sorted.'

'By Christmas Day?'

'I don't know. It's only the day after tomorrow.'

'You promised!' she wailed. In some ways she was still a baby.

'I know. But time is tight.'

'What about my present?'

See what I mean about being a baby? 'It's safe,' I said.

'Where?'

'At the flat, of course.'

'And Christmas dinner?'

'I'm not sure.'

'You promised.'

'I know, love. But it's difficult.'

'Oh, Dad. I'll have no one.'

'There's Auntie Jane and Uncle Joe.'

'She's not Mum. And he's not you.' And she started to cry. Loud sobs that almost ripped my heart out of my chest.

'Darling,' I said. 'I'll try. I promise.'

'No you won't.' And she slammed the phone down.

I saw Robber's face when I disconnected. 'Family problems?' he said.

I tossed the phone to him and said, 'Tell me about it. Sometimes I think I'd be better off without one.'

57

'What are you going to do about her?' asked Robber.

'I'll call her in the morning. She'll come round. She always does. Or at least she always did. But she's at a difficult age.'

'Who isn't? Listen, Sharman. Why don't you just take all this to the authorities?'

'The police? I don't think so. They'd lock me up and throw away the key. They'd love to have me in custody for a cop killing. They wouldn't listen to a word I said.'

'I'd come with you. Explain.'

'Fuck off, Jack. You don't know any more than they do. It's just my word against nothing.'

'But I'd do it.'

'What? And miss your Christmas bonus?' I looked at the case.

He looked at it too and shook his head. 'The odds are bad.'

'Come on, Jack. I can remember when you'd love to go in and break a few spades' heads.'

'Ah yes. But then I had the might of the Met behind me.'

'I'm not giving up Tootsie,' I said grimly. 'That dude is mine. I don't really care about the rest. But Tootsie and his mates are going down. Large.'

'You're crazy.'

'And tired. I need some sleep, man. I feel like I haven't closed my eyes for a week.'

'OK,' said Robber. 'Sleep on it. That's a good idea. We'll talk more in the morning.'

'Christmas Eve,' I said. 'Goodwill to all men.'

He smiled and we got up, switched off the lights and hit the wooden hill to Bedfordshire as Judith would've put it when she was little. God alone knows what she calls it now.

The bed was comfortable and the sheets were fresh and smelled of spring mornings, but I couldn't sleep for a long time. My head was full of exploding aeroplanes and dead bodies littered about like autumn leaves in a Vauxhall tunnel.

But eventually, as a distant clock struck four, I fell into a restless sleep.

58

Christmas Eve morning

The church clock woke me again. It was still dark. I counted eight strokes. I'd been dreaming about shooting people. I didn't know who, or if it was a dream about the past or a premonition of the future. There was a tap on the door and Nellie brought me in a cup of hot, sweet tea. It's little kindnesses like that that make the world go round. I couldn't remember the last time someone brought me tea in bed. Then I did. It had been Dawn. My wife. I didn't want to think about that. The widow seemed happy. Robber must've paid our rent in kind. 'Jack's up,' she said. 'He's having breakfast.'

'I'll be down directly,' I said.

After she'd gone I drank my tea, got up, found the bathroom, did what I could to myself without aid of a razor, got dressed in clothes that were sour to say the least, and went downstairs.

Robber was at the dining-room table finishing his eggs and bacon. He looked up when I went in and wrinkled his nose. 'You stink,' he said.

'So would you if you'd been wearing the same clothes for . . .' I hesitated. I couldn't remember. 'Christ knows how long,' I finished.

'Sure,' he said.

Nellie stuck her head round the door. 'Breakfast?' she said to me.

'Please.'

'Egg, bacon, sausage, tomato?'

'Thanks.'

'I'll get you some toast. Tea or coffee?'

'Tea please,' I said, and she withdrew.

'Good billet,' said Robber.

'Yes,' I agreed.

'Right,' he said, pushing his plate away. 'What are we going to do?'

'I'm going to phone Judith. Then we take a cruise round. I need to think.'

'And that's never been easy.'

'Cheers, Jack,' I said.

The widow brought my breakfast and a fresh pot of strong tea. Robber had been out and got the Sunday papers. I wasn't featured, but the boys from Vauxhall were. I reminded myself to get rid of the Detonics as soon as this was all over. If I survived, that was. If I didn't, it wouldn't matter.

When I'd eaten, I borrowed Robber's mobile again and called Jane's house. She answered. 'Nick,' she said. 'What the hell is going on?'

'Save it, Jane,' I replied. 'It's all on the news. Is Judith there?'

'She's in bed.'

'Haul her out, will you? We had a ruck last night.'

'You can't get on with anyone, can you?' she said and plonked the receiver down with a bang.

She was back within a minute and her voice had changed. It was edged with panic as she said, 'Nick, she's not there!'

'What?'

'Her bed's not been slept in.'

'What?'

'Stop saying that. She's gone.'

'Jesus Christ on a crutch,' I said. 'Where is she?'

'How the hell do I know? You spoke to her last. What did you say?'

'That I might not be able to make Christmas dinner and that her present was at the flat ... Fuck,' I said. 'I bet she's gone there to get it,' and I cut off Jane without saying goodbye.

59

'Come on, Jack,' I said. 'Get your shit together. We've got to get out of here.'

He got up from the table and went upstairs. When he came back he was wearing his coat, which had an unmistakable bulge under the left armpit, and was carrying his car keys. 'I'm fit,' he said. 'Let's go.'

In the hall, we said goodbye to the widow. Robber gave her an awkward hug and said, 'See you later, Nellie.'

'Be careful, Jack,' she replied.

'Thanks for everything,' I said and touched her hand.

'You'll be back,' she said.

'I hope so,' and I pecked her on the cheek, and Robber and I went out into the bitter, misty morning which it seemed might turn out to be our last.

We climbed into the Morris Traveller, which was coated with a thin layer of ice and whose inside was colder than a deep freeze. I stashed the bag of dope behind the front seats and Robber ground the starter. The motor caught on the third try and he wiped the inside of the windscreen with one hand. 'Give it a minute to warm up,' he said, putting on the demister which had about as much breath as a duck with asthma.

'Come on, Jack,' I said impatiently. 'We've got to get rolling.'

'Patience,' he said, as the windscreen slowly cleared and he pushed in the choke and selected first gear. 'It needs time.'

'Which is one thing we don't have,' I said.

Robber eased the clutch out and with a hop, skip and jump the Morris moved off.

We headed up Knights Hill into Norwood Road and turned left at the railway bridge into my street. The car was beginning to warm up by then and the heater started to cope with the cold. 'Cruise it, Jack,' I said. 'There might be someone watching the house.'

'I doubt it. It's Christmas Eve. Everyone will want to be off duty. And them's that are on are getting ready for tonight's punch-ups.'

'I hope you're right,' I said. 'But if there is someone watching and Judith's gone there, at least she'll be safe with them.'

Robber let the old car drift round the side streets and I clocked every motor for copperish-looking occupants, but there were none. Once satisfied, I told him to stop three or four houses up from where I had my flat.

He parked the car and I said, 'You can stay here if you like.'

'I'll come with you. Who else is likely to be at home?'

'No one. There's three flats in the house. The big one in the middle is empty, waiting to be sold. And the girl at the bottom always goes home at Christmas to see her folks in Bolton.'

'Good,' he said. 'At least we'll have some privacy. Come on, let's go.'

We both got out of the car, opening our coats for easy access to our weapons, and walked together to the house. 'Judith's got a key, I take it?' said Robber.

I nodded as we walked across the empty forecourt to the porch. I had my key in my hand but I didn't need it. The massive old front door was open an inch with the latch back.

'Shit,' I said, taking out the Detonics and cocking the hammer. 'Jack, I don't like this one little bit.'

60

Slowly, I pushed the front door open to its full extent. The hall beyond was empty. I crept in silently and Robber followed, pulling his massive Smith from under his coat as he came. I gestured for silence and led the way up the stairs. The door to the middle flat was secure and I headed towards my apartment. I flattened myself on the last flight of steps and realized something was wrong. The normally gloomy hallway was too light. I raised my head until my eyes were level with the landing above and saw why. The door to my flat had been smashed down and lay inside the living room. 'Shit,' I said silently and slid upwards and across the carpet. Ducking down to make a smaller target, and with the Detonics fanning the air in front of me, I peered into my flat. It was empty, as far as I could see, but someone had done a good job of trashing the place.

'Shit,' I said again, a bit louder this time as I went inside, checking the small kitchen and bathroom beyond. Empty again. 'Come on in, Jack,' I said. 'The birds have flown.'

Robber followed me inside and said, 'You sure?'

I nodded. 'Not much room here to hide,' I said. 'Look at this fucking mess.' Someone had been through the place like a whirlwind, and I kicked at a pile of CDs that had been scattered across the floor.

'That's not going to improve the look of the place,' said

Robber. 'But then it's not going to do it much harm, considering the usual state of your housekeeping.'

'Judith's been here,' I said.

'How do you know?'

I gestured towards the bed. Bunched up on top was a sheet of Christmas wrapping. 'Her present,' I said. I pulled the bed away from the wall and behind it was the pair of rollerblade boots. 'And she didn't take them. So that means someone took her. I'd lay money on it.'

'I hope you're wrong,' said Robber. And as if on cue, the phone, which miraculously had survived the pillage, began to ring.

61

I picked up the receiver. 'Sharman?' said a voice I didn't recognize, although it had a faint Caribbean lilt, even on a single word.

'Yeah?'

'Where you been, man? We been looking for you.'

'I've been around.'

'Sure. Now listen up, man. You've got something we want, and we've got something you want.'

'What?'

'Look around yourself, man. You've had visitors. What do you think? Don't play games. She's young, she's sweet.'

'You bastard.'

'No bad language, man. Now we want to do a deal with you. Do as you're told and no one gets hurt.'

'Let me speak to her.'

'All in good time. You were very unwise to let her wander the streets alone. It's a bad neighbourhood.'

'If you hurt her . . .'

'No threats, man. Don't be foolish. You got a mobile?'

'No . . . Yeah.'

'Make up your mind.'

'Yes,' I said.

'Gimme the number.'

I looked at Robber and covered the mouthpiece. 'What's the number of your phone? Come on, quick.'

He reeled off the number and I repeated it to the caller. 'Goodbye now,' he said. 'We'll call you back.'

'I want to . . .' But he cut me off.

I slammed down the phone. 'Fuckers have got Judith,' I said.

I would've tried 1471, but where I live doesn't have that service. We've not been digitalized and our telephone lines are still strung from wooden poles. And I ain't joking. 'Who was it?' said Robber. 'Any idea?'

'Some black bastard,' I said. 'Could've been with Mr B., Darkman or Tootsie. Or anybody. I didn't recognize the voice.'

'You sure they've got her?'

'No. But it's a good assumption. Whoever it was knew that the place had been turned over. And knew she'd been here.'

'Then we'd better start looking,' said Robber.

'They want the dope, whoever they are,' I said.

'I just bet they do.'

'What do you think about that?'

'We'll do what we have to do.'

'If we give it up, you'll miss your Christmas box.'

'Then we'll try not to give it up. But, if it means getting Judith back, we'll do it. As long as we're sure that we do get her back.'

I suddenly felt terribly cold. 'We'd better,' I said.

'We will. I take it they're going to call on the mobile?'

I nodded.

'Where do we start?' he asked.

'In alphabetical order. Mr B., I think. It was his gear in the first place.'

'He'll welcome you with open arms, then.'

'I very much doubt that.'

'We'll have to see, won't we?'

'Yeah.'

'Come on, let's go.'

'Wait a minute, I could use a clean shirt.'

'You're telling me.'

I took a few seconds to find one amid the debris, took off Parker's coat, which I dropped on the floor and slid into the shirt and my leather jacket, that was on the bed with the pockets pulled inside out. I felt better for that. More ready for action. Finally I slid the Detonics into my belt and zipped the jacket up over it. 'Come on then, Sharman,' said Robber. 'Time's a-wasting.'

His enthusiasm depressed me. The last place I wanted to go was back to Mr B.'s. I mean, talk about Daniel and the lion's den. This beat that little story hands down.

62

We went back to the car and drove to Brixton. We were there in less than ten minutes. Although a lot of shops and stores were open for Christmas Eve, the streets were deserted as though Christmas Day had come twenty-four hours early. The freezing mist persisted, and I shivered even though the car's heater was blowing warm air. It could've been the weather, but more likely it was the fear of what might be happening to Judith, and anger and frustration that I couldn't help her. I flexed my fingers as if I was pointing a gun at the head of the cocksucker who had taken her. And if I had been, and they'd hurt her, I knew I'd use it. If only . . .

As we drove I looked out for anyone watching us, but came up blank. Still, someone had to be or else they wouldn't have known that Robber and I had gone to the flat. Or maybe they'd just kept trying the phone on the off chance.

I got Robber to park three or four streets away from Mr B.'s place after we drove past and eyeballed the house. It was as quiet as the grave. I left the bag of dope and my gun in the car with him. There was no point going in armed. If Mr B. was holding Judith I didn't want to start a shooting war. And if he wasn't, there was no point anyway. If they let me out again they'd just keep it and we'd be one weapon down. And if they didn't let me out, well, then I was dead and it wouldn't matter. 'I don't know what's going to go down,' I said, before I got out of the Morris. 'We didn't part on the best of terms and I nicked his dope. At least I can use that as a bargaining tool. That is, if he doesn't shoot first and ask questions after.'

'You're taking a big chance,' said Robber.

'Don't I know it. But what else can I do? Christ knows what's happening to Judith.' It didn't bear thinking about. 'But if anything does . . . Trust me, somehow I'll take some of those fuckers with me.'

'How long should I give you?'

'What? Before you come in with six guns blazing like bloody John Wayne? Give it up, Robber. If I'm not back within an hour, you might as well flog off the drugs and forget you ever knew me. I'll be brown bread and that's all there is to it.'

'Police?' he asked again.

'After all your experience you still have a touching faith in law and order,' I said. 'No. My ex-sister-in-law will have that covered. Leave it to her. Just keep that mobile phone of yours switched on. If Mr B. has got Judith he isn't likely to get in touch whilst I'm inside his house. But if someone else has her they might. Just say I'll be around later or else all bets are off. Unless, of course, you want to swap the dope for her. How altruistic are you, Jack? How much is one little girl's life worth to you?'

He looked at me hard. 'I just don't know about you, Sharman,' he said. 'No wonder you never lasted in the Job.'

'I don't work well in group situations,' I replied. 'I'm too much of a loner.'

'But you were glad enough to see me last night.'

'There's always exceptions, Jack,' I said, and touched his arm.

He put his hand on mine and said, 'Good luck, son. Take it easy, eh?'

'I'll try. At least I never shot his fish.'

'Do what?'

'Long story. See you later, I hope.'

And with that, I got out of the car and angled across the street in the direction of Mr B.'s and whatever I'd find there.

63

I opened the gate to Mr B.'s house, walked up the path bordered with browned out, skeletal plants waiting for spring to coat them with green, and rang the front doorbell. I only had to wait ten seconds before it was opened by Harold, and Goldie and Majesty appeared from the side of the house. I might've guessed there was a video monitor somewhere and they'd watched me arrive. There were no weapons visible, but I knew they were close and I lifted my arms away from my body to show that I wasn't carrying. Harold grabbed me by the shoulder and pulled me into the hall where he frisked me thoroughly. Goldie and Majesty hustled in after me and closed the door behind them. Somewhere above us I could hear The Jimi Hendrix Experience cranked up on a stereo, 'If Six was Nine', and it occurred to me that if six *was* nine, life would be a very different experience altogether.

When Harold was satisfied I was clean he put his face close to mine. So close that I felt his warm breath on my cheek and smelled mint where he'd been chewing gum, when he whispered, 'Glad you came back, mon, but *you* won't be. The boss wants to talk to you big time. You must be crazy coming back here after what you did.'

'I want to talk to him too,' I replied. 'Someone's taken my daughter.'

'To a party?' asked Harold. 'To a club? Out shopping? What?'

'Kidnapped her,' I said, controlling my temper with an effort. I wasn't in the mood for his wit. Especially if he knew where she was.

'Couldn't've happened to a nicer guy,' he said. 'Come on. Mr B.'s waiting. And he ain't a happy man.'

He took me by the upper arm and walked me fast towards the back of the house and Mr B.'s lair. I tried to shake off his hand but he just gripped my biceps harder.

The door to the office was closed and Harold hit it hard, still pushing me in front of him, and when it burst open I saw that Mr B. was alone, the lenses of his dark glasses catching the light from the aquaria, making his eyes look as if they were floating underwater.

'Mr Sharman,' he said. 'We meet again, and so soon. Believe me, this is more of a pleasure for me than you'll ever know.'

64

'I wish I could say the same,' I said.

Harold gave me a dig in the back. I was beginning to dislike him intensely. 'Was he armed?' Mr B. asked him.

'No.'

'Wise. And the merchandise?'

'No.'

'You have something I want,' Mr B. said to me. 'Where is it?'

'I could say the same to you,' I said.

'I don't understand,' said Mr B., and I saw his brow wrinkle through the gloom.

'My daughter,' I said. 'Her name's Judith. She's fifteen, and her mum died just over a week ago.'

'Yes?'

'Do you have her?'

'Why should I?'

'Someone trashed my flat last night, or early this morning. She was there. They took her. They want the dope in exchange. Whoever called me told me the news was black. Hey, guess what? I put two and two together and immediately thought of you. I'm a detective, remember?'

'I don't know what you're talking about.'

'I'd expect you to say that.'

'Then you're not disappointed, are you? Mr Sharman, I can assure you I know nothing of the whereabouts of your daughter.'

'What about the rest of the Pump House Gang? Harold?'

'No, mon. We never snatched the kid. But hey, maybe she'd like being round the brothers. They'd probably be honoured to show her a good time. Big dicks, get me?'

Everything that had happened over the past week or so boiled up in me then, and I let go with a roundhouse right that connected perfectly with the side of his jaw, and I swear he went cross-eyed as he went down and hit the carpet with a thump. He lay there, breathing hoarsely. I turned to Mr B., shaking my hand where I reckoned I'd busted at least one knuckle, and said, 'If I'd had a gun I'd've shot him.'

'I believe you would,' said Mr B., and showed me the gun that he'd kept on his lap. 'But you're not going to get another chance to point a pistol at me.'

'You going to shoot me?' I asked. 'I never shot your fish.'

'And that's the one reason you're alive now, and will continue to be until your mouth or your fists come up against someone less forgiving.'

Just then Goldie and Majesty burst into the room toting a matching pair of Browning niners, once again the weapon of choice of the discerning black gangster. Mr B. must've pressed the panic button. 'Whoa,' I said, raising my hands. 'Don't shoot. There's innocent fish in here.'

'Take him upstairs to cool his heels,' said Mr B., 'before I decide what to do with him. And come back and get Harold and wake him up.'

65

'Listen, I'd love to stay and chat,' I said. 'But my daughter's still missing. And if she's not here, I've got to get out on the street and find her.'

'Really,' said Mr B. 'And you think I'm just going to let you walk out of here, just like that? You still have what belongs to me, remember?'

'Then you'll have to kill me, here and now. And then you'll get nothing.'

He thought about it for a second. 'That's how it's going to have to be then,' he said.

'You bastard.'

'No. I have a birth certificate. My mother and father were married.'

'Listen. I know you've got a down on me, but my daughter's

just fifteen. She's never hurt anyone in her life.' I was beginning to get desperate. 'Give *her* a chance at least. Whoever's got her will kill her unless I come across with the dope.'

'My dope.'

'Who the fuck cares?' I shouted. 'There's plenty more where that came from, and besides, you'll never see it again if I don't walk out of here in one piece.'

He pondered again. 'So what do you suggest?' he asked.

I was sweating through my clothes by then. 'Look,' I said. 'Give me one of your men and a fast car, and the other guns that Harold took off me. I'm expecting a call from whoever's got Judith. I've got a partner. He's out there with a portable phone and the dope. We go and pick him up. Your man stays with me until we can track down who's got Judith. Then we pretend to negotiate and take the bastards out. They're as much your enemies as they are mine. My guess is that it's Tootsie, but I don't know for certain. It could be anyone, and it's as much in your interests as it is in mine to find out. They're taking the piss out of you, Mr B. Dissing you, big time. Listen, I'm begging you. I don't care about myself. It's Judith I care about. Have some humanity, man. It's only money to you. To me it's my only child.'

Mr B. thought some more. 'I must be crazy,' he said. 'But I'll do it. But you have to take Harold.'

Oh shit, I thought. He was coming round by then, sitting in a chair that Majesty had helped him to. 'He doesn't like me,' I said.

'I don't care about that,' said Mr B. 'I just want my merchandise back. You take Harold and your guns and the BMW and find out who is working against me. It's time there was a showdown. There are too many warring gangs round

176

here for my liking. The whole set-up is beginning to vex me. I have to show people who's top dog. Maybe you were sent to settle the matter once and for all. But don't try and make a fool of me or you'll regret it. Maybe I'm getting soft in my old age, but things need to be sorted. Now get out of my sight. I have to feed my fish.'

66

'I ain't going nowhere with that piece of shit,' said Harold.

'You'll do as you're told,' said Mr B. 'Who the hell do you think you are?'

'Fucker cold-cocked me.'

'It served you right. You should have been more aware.'

'Motherfucker.'

Mr B. said, 'Majesty, take Mr Sharman out the back. Goldie. You go with them. Harold. You stay here. We've got things to talk about.'

I was kicking my heels in the kitchen when Harold came in carrying a small sports bag. There was a bruise on his jaw and the skin was swollen and tender-looking. 'Hello, Harold,' I said. 'Nasty hickey you've got there.'

'It'll all even out,' he replied. 'In the fullness of time.' And he touched one hand to the sore spot. 'You could've broken my jaw.'

'It wasn't for the want of trying. Any more cracks about my daughter and next time I will.'

'In your dreams, Sharman.'

'You coming with us?'

Harold nodded.

'Mr B. made you see sense, huh? No point in arguing with the boss.'

'Bollocks.'

'You got something for me?' I asked.

He dropped the bag on the table with a thud and gestured for me to open it. Inside were Lopez's .45 auto and Latimer's Colt revolver. They were both loaded and I stashed them away out of sight. 'What you got?' I asked. 'This could get ugly.'

Harold was wearing the same mac as the night I'd met him at Victoria and he pulled it open to show the Mini-Uzi hanging from his shoulder by a leather strap, the thirty-shot magazine jutted obscenely from the butt. 'Good job,' I said. 'Just remember whose side you're on.'

'My side and Mr B.'s,' he said back. 'Now come on, let's go.'

So we went.

We took the black Beemer and drove round to where the Morris Traveller was still parked, a puff of smoke coming from the exhaust where Robber had left the engine running. On the way I checked to see that we weren't being followed. Harold stopped the car and we got out and walked over. I saw Robber's face, white through the windscreen, and I held up my hands placatingly. He wound down the window and I saw the Smith in his hand. 'We come in peace,' I said. 'This is Harold, I told you about him.'

'Harold Amidon,' said Robber. 'Hello, Harold. I didn't realize it was you. How are you keeping?'

'I thought you'd gone away,' said Harold.

'I came back.'

'You two know each other?' I asked.

''Course we do,' said Robber. 'How long was it, Harold? Eighteen months' youth custody? I see you haven't mended your ways. Still mixing with bad company.'

'This is going from bad to worse,' said Harold.

'What happened to your face?' said Robber. 'Walk into a door?'

'Long story,' said Harold.

'Has your phone rung?' I asked Robber, interrupting any more reminiscences and idle chit-chat.

Robber shook his head, and then, as if on cue, the phone started to trill musically on the passenger seat next to him.

67

It was the same male voice as before. 'Hi, Sharman,' he said. 'How they hangin'?'

'Where's my daughter?'

'She cool man. Don't worry.'

'Let me talk to her.'

'Maybe later.'

'Maybe now. Or I take what I've got that you want and drop it in the Thames.'

'You wouldn't be that foolish.'

'Try me, blood.'

'Then she'd die.'

'And you'd be a dead man walking. But for all I know she's dead now. Or maybe you don't have her at all.'

'We do.'

'Then let me speak to her.'

'OK, man.'

There was a pause, then I recognized Judith's voice and relief went through me like a river. 'Daddy,' she said, 'come and get me please.'

'Are you all right?'

'Yes. But they're horrible.'

'Where are . . . ?'

But the phone was snatched away from her and the voice said, 'You ready to deal?'

'I am.'

'Good. I'll call you later, man. This is something best done when the sun has gone down. Stay by the phone. Bye now.'

And he was gone.

68

Harold and I climbed into the Morris and I told him and Robber what had transpired on the dog. Harold sneered at the inside of the old motor, but his eyes lit up when he saw the case full of dope. 'Still no idea who it was?' said Robber.

'No. But I think we can strike Mr B. off the list,' I replied.

'Well, that's something. And what's young Harold doing here?' Robber again.

'He's our minder. Or rather the merchandise's minder. Mr B. wasn't too keen on letting me out of his sight, but I convinced him that he'd never see it again if he didn't let me go.'

'How true,' said Robber. 'Well, Harold, whoever would've thought it? You taking care of me, instead of me taking care of you.'

'Just one of life's little ironies,' replied the black man.

'So, what next?' Robber asked me.

'Darkman. Though I think it's Tootsie who's at the bottom of this. I'm just not too keen on trying to get inside his place. He'll be waiting after what happened yesterday. And loaded for bear.'

'Darkman it is, then,' said Robber.

'We'll take the BMW,' I said. 'Leave your car here.'

'Good job,' said Harold. 'I don't want to be seen driving in this heap.'

'It's a good car,' said Robber defensively. 'My sister's had it since new.'

'Should be in a museum,' said Harold.

'I'd like to see that Krautmobile of yours still going after a hundred thousand miles.'

'Can we save the road test till later?' I asked. 'Remember what's at stake here.'

'Sorry,' said Robber and we got out of the Traveller and went over to the BMW and climbed aboard. We put the case in the boot. I sat in the back, out of the way. I was still amongst Britain's most wanted and I didn't want to be recognized by some passing copper. Especially with what we were carrying in the motor.

We shot over to Deptford fast, with Harold playing his jungle through the car's big speakers and Robber constantly turning the volume down. It was mid-morning by then and the mist had cleared slightly, but it was still cold and miserable, and people were mostly staying close to home.

We left the car on the edge of the Lion Estate and walked through to Darkman's block and climbed the stairs. We took the case with us. It would be just my luck for some chancer to nick the car whilst we were gone.

I hammered on the metal door of Darkman's flat, but there was no answer.

'You want we should go in?' said Harold.

'Metal doors,' I said. 'Metal grilles on the windows.'

'Check this,' he said, and brought out a wicked-looking, short crowbar from under his coat.

'You came prepared,' I said.

'That's my job.'

'What do you reckon, Jack?' I said.

'Seems a shame to go without paying our respects,' he replied.

'OK,' I said. 'Do it.'

Harold looked up and down the balcony, but all was serene. And even if it hadn't been, the occupants of the Lion had seen worse. He forced the edge of the crowbar between the door and the jamb and leaned his weight on it. There was a terrible squeal of metal on metal when the door began to give, and with an exhalation of breath, Harold pushed harder and the door popped.

'Well done,' I said.

'He got a dog?' asked Harold.

'I don't think so,' I replied.

But even so, Harold whistled and called out 'Here, boy,' before he led the way in.

It was dark inside and he fumbled for a light switch and ignited the weak bulb in the ceiling socket.

The flat was in the same state as it had been a few days before, but this time it was empty. 'Shit,' I said when we'd been through the place, guns drawn. 'I wonder where the hell the little bastard's got to?'

69

'Fuck this,' I said when we'd finished turning the place over. 'This is getting us nowhere. My daughter's being held by some crazy spades, Christ knows where, and Christ knows what they're doing to her. And all we're doing is poncing around London like three spare pricks at a wedding.' I could feel the tension in my every nerve-ending. If something didn't happen soon, I was going to burst.

'I've never been no spare prick, even at a wedding,' declared Harold. 'And less of the "crazy spades".'

'Be quiet, Harold,' I said. 'Or I'll hit you again.'

'You'd better not try, brother, or I'll hose you down with this,' and he tapped the barrel of the Uzi.

'And I'll hose you down with this,' said Robber, brandishing the S&W .44 magnum. 'You want to make my day, punk?' Carrying that gun, I knew Robber would have to spout that line sooner or later.

Harold turned the Uzi on Robber. 'In your dreams.'

Robber cocked the Smith. Things were going from bad to worse, and I didn't want to be caught in the crossfire.

'Play nicely, boys,' I said. 'We're supposed to be on the same side, remember?'

'Just temporarily,' said Harold to me after a moment, and he lowered the machine pistol. 'When we ain't, you and me gonna talk.'

'I'll look forward to it,' I said. 'Robber.'

Robber scowled, but let down the hammer of his gun carefully, and I breathed a sigh of relief.

'So what the fuck do we do now?' I asked no one in particular.

'Wait for the phone to ring,' said Robber.

And of course it did.

70

Christmas Eve afternoon

And of course it was Robber's sister checking up to see how he was. 'I'm all right doll,' he said. 'Sound as a pound. I don't know when I'll be back. Tomorrow, probably. Now can you get off the line? I'm waiting for an important call.'

'No. Not more important than yours.' He reddened as he listened. 'Come on, doll, have a heart ... No. No, I'll call you. Yes. Soon.' And he cut her off.

'Who was that? Your mum?' asked Harold. 'You been staying out late again?'

'Shut your cake-hole or I'll shut it for you,' barked Robber. 'Don't you mention my mum.'

Robber was very sensitive about his mother. I remember the day she died. I'd almost died that day too, and I'd never let Robber forget it.

'Cut it out, you two,' I said. I felt a bit like a mother myself by then. A mother with a pair of fractious toddlers, trying to get round Tesco's without strangling them. 'Let's get out of here and scout round Tootsie's. She's got to be there ... Shit I don't know. But let's go and have a squint anyway.'

On the way we stopped for something to eat. Harold parked

the Beemer outside a McDonalds' in Peckham and he and Robber went inside. They brought me back a Big Mac, fries and a Coke, and although I was starving, I couldn't eat more than a mouthful. I was too worried about Judith and everything else that had gone off. I drank the Coke and threw the rest back in the bag and left it on the floor of the car.

Then Harold took us on a tour of Tootsie's establishments. All was quiet, and we didn't try and go inside any of them. It was too risky. We weren't mob-handed enough, and even if Tootsie was holding Judith, we didn't know exactly where. I was getting more and more pissed off with every passing moment.

The phone rang again at three as it was just getting dark and a cold wind came up, dispersing the mist and bringing in heavy grey clouds full of snow that closed in over London.

'Sharman. You ready?' said the voice I'd come to recognize.

'Is Judith OK?' I asked.

'Fit as a flea.'

'If you've touched her . . .'

'Man. We don't want her body. She's too scrawny. All we want is what's in that bag you got.'

'Let me speak to her.'

There was a pause, then Judith came on. She sounded tearful and frightened and my heart went out to her. 'Daddy? How much longer?' she said.

'Not long. Are you all right?'

'Fine. Just come and get me.'

'Soon,' I assured her, and the bloke came back on.

'Talk to me,' I said.

'Five o'clock tonight. Get yourself down to Clapham. We meet on the common at the back of The Windmill pub. You know it?'

'Sure.'

'Right. Park up on the road that runs past the lake. What you driving?'

'A silver BMW Alpine.'

There was a pause. 'Where'd you get that?' he asked suspiciously.

'I borrowed it off a friend.'

'Would that friend be Mr B. by any chance?'

'Yeah.'

'So you're not alone?'

It was pointless to lie. 'No.'

'Be alone, or the deal's off. Park as close to the pub as you can. Leave the headlights on and stand by the car. We'll find you.'

'And?'

'And we do a swap. Simple, man. Just be there unarmed and solo. Otherwise you looking at a firefight, brother. A firefight I promise you won't survive. Or your little girl. Five o'clock. Be there. And no fucking tricks.'

And he rang off again.

71

I told Robber and Harold what had occurred, and Harold said, 'We can go and get the rest of the boys. Get them tooled up.'

'We're talking about my daughter's life here,' I said. 'No way, Harold. I'm not risking her getting caught in the crossfire.'

'So what do we do then?'

'We do exactly what we're told. You two make yourselves scarce and I swap the drugs for Judith.'

'Mr B. won't be pleased.'

'Fuck Mr B.,' I said. 'And the horse he rode in on. We do what we're told. You two can piss off into the boozer. I wait by the car with the stuff and do the business.'

'What happens if they take the dope and keep her?' asked Harold.

'Why should they? Once they've got the stuff, her value is zero.' At least I hoped it was. What Harold suggested was too dreadful to contemplate.

'I don't trust them, whoever they are,' said Robber.

'I don't trust them either,' I said. 'But what can we do? We have to take their word they'll do what they say.'

'You spoke to her?' Robber again.

'Yeah.'

'She sounded OK?'

'Frightened, but I don't think they've hurt her, if that's what you mean.'

'That's exactly what I mean.'

'No,' I shook my head. 'I'd know. She wouldn't be able to hide that.'

'Well that's something, at least,' said Robber.

'I think I should tell Mr B.,' said Harold.

'Harold,' I said. 'You don't tell Mr B. anything. You shtum up. You can tell him all about it after.'

'But what about the dope?'

'Fuck the dope,' I said, feeling as if my head was about to explode. 'Listen, Harold. When we've done the exchange we'll have a good idea who's got the stuff and then you can go in team-handed and get it back if you want. You've done it once, what's to stop you doing it again? But for now you will drive to Clapham and find a place to park up.'

72

We got to Clapham Common before four. Harold took a left into Windmill Drive that runs between the South Circ and Clapham Common South Side and parked facing the main road, as close as possible to what the geezer on the phone had described as the lake, but in fact was just a pond. Eagle Pond, in fact, trivia fans. It was fully dark by then and there were only a few lights on the drive. The clouds had lowered, the wind had dropped, a few snowflakes fell from the midnight-coloured sky and ice had formed at the edge of the water. It was freezing cold and miserable, and I felt about as depressed as it's possible to be without finishing it all.

Harold left the engine running to keep the heater going and said, 'What now?'

'Now you two go and warm your feet by the fire in the pub and have a drink. I stay here with the dope and Jack's phone – and my guns, just in case – and with any luck by five past five we can all go about our various business.'

'You're coming with me to tell Mr B. what went down,' said Harold. 'I ain't gonna be the one to explain. I ain't gonna be the one to feel the heat of his wrath.' Harold could be almost biblical at times.

'Whatever you want, Harold,' I said. 'Just as long as Judith is safe.'

He shook his head and sighed, and Robber said, 'Come on,

Harold. I'm dying for a pint. And with a bit of luck they might have some hot mince pies in there.' He always was a great man for his stomach, was Robber.

They both got out of the car and I called Robber back and said, 'Don't let him use the phone and if he goes to the khazi, go with him.' I saw his face in the reflection from the dashboard. 'Don't worry about all that, Jack. Just do it. He's probably got a mobile on him somewhere and I don't want a posse of heavily armed spades turning up here and ruining everything.'

'OK, Sharman,' he said. 'And you be careful, you hear?'

'I hear you,' I said, and I watched enviously as they walked towards the beckoning lights of The Windmill, and I settled down to wait.

73

Christmas Eve evening

I turned off the lights but left the engine running to keep the heater going, tuned the radio into a funk station and watched the world go by. Not that much of it did. Just the occasional civilian walking the dog, a few punters going into the boozer, and the cars on the main road in front of me, their tyres hissing on the pavement.

At five to five the phone rang. It was the kidnapper. 'You alone?' he asked.

'Yeah.'

'Put the headlights on full beam, get out of the car with the stuff, and wait.'

189

I did as I was told, holding the case in front of me in full sight.

At five o'clock precisely a dark-coloured Ford Scorpio rumbled out of the darkness. It had tinted windows, so I couldn't see inside, but I knew this was the one.

It drew up next to me, facing towards the South Circular, and simultaneously the driver's and the rear passenger's windows ran down. The driver was the big black guy I'd met at Darkman's flat and behind him sat another spade, one I'd never seen before, and who I assumed was my anonymous caller. Next to him I saw Judith's blonde hair and pale, drawn face. Of the Darkman there was no sign.

'You alone?' said the mysterious passenger again, and I recognized his voice as the geezer on the phone.

'Yeah?'

'No one in the car?'

'No.'

'That the stuff?' He nodded at the case.

'Yeah.'

'Show.'

I opened it wide enough for him to see the dope in the reflection from the Beemer's headlights.

'Give.'

'Let my daughter go first.'

'Girl,' he said, and she opened the door on the other side of the Ford.

This was the bad moment. The actual exchange. Where if anything was going to go wrong it would.

And it did. Big time.

As I was about to hand in the case and Judith was halfway out of the car, the driver said, 'You sure there's no one in the car?'

"Course I am,' I replied, as the guy in the back took the case from my hands.

'Hope so,' said the driver and hauled out a stubby, short-barrelled TEC-22 and sprayed the Beemer with 9mm bullets.

'*Motherfucker*,' I said, jumping sideways to avoid the slugs that cannoned off the car as the bullets shot sparks from the metalwork and the petrol tank blew, nearly knocking me over, and the case hit the road and bounced into the gutter.

Then, out of nowhere, Harold arrived, the Mini-Uzi in his hands, and he started to fire at the Ford, bullets ripping into the back end.

'*No!*' I screamed, as Judith ducked down. 'No, you stupid prat! Stop!'

Robber was behind him, the S&W in his fist.

I clawed for the Detonics in my belt as the Ford's driver turned the TEC on Harold and Robber, stitching a line of holes across Harold's chest and knocking Robber off his feet, as the guy in the back threw himself across the seat, grabbed Judith and dragged her back into the Ford as the driver put his foot down and the Scorpio fishtailed away with a screech from the back tyres.

I stood in the flickering light of the burning BMW, gun in hand, and looked at the carnage. Harold was making horrible sucking noises from the wounds in his chest and Robber was rolling on the ground, clutching at his thigh where a bullet, or more likely a ricochet, from the look of the wound, had hit him.

I ran over and knelt beside him. 'Not again,' he said. 'Get a fucking ambulance!'

I did as he told me, keying 999 into his mobile. 'Ambulance,' I said when the operator answered. 'Windmill Pub,

Clapham Common. Two men down with bullet wounds. One serious, one not so bad.'

'Your name please,' said the operator calmly, as if that sort of thing happened every day, which in south London was truer than most people imagined.

'Just do it,' I said and cut her off.

'Are you OK?' I said to Robber.

'Stupid fucking question,' he said through white lips. 'I couldn't stop him.'

'Well he paid for it,' I said, looking at Harold's prone body.

'Go,' said Robber. 'Get out of here.'

'But . . .'

'But nothing. There's nothing you can do. Go.'

I stood and looked round. The Beemer was out of the game, still burning merrily, and a crowd had gathered outside the pub to watch the fun, some still with drinks in their hands. Less than twenty yards away in the car park a bloke was standing, one foot inside the driver's door of a new Vauxhall Omega, the keys hanging from one finger. It wasn't my car of choice, but beggars can't be choosers, so I stood and ran towards him. I left Harold's Uzi, which was hopelessly tangled up in his coat, but picked up Robber's magnum, which I stuck into the pocket of my jacket where its weight dragged the material down, then grabbed the case of dope from where it had fallen. Too late, the geezer with the Vauxhall realized what was happening and made to get into the car. 'Stop!' I said. He did, with a look of surprise on his fat face. 'Gimme the keys,' I demanded.

'Not my car,' he said. 'I just got it for Christmas.'

'Hope it's run in,' I said as I took the keys, pushed him aside, threw the Detonics, the case and the mobile on to the passenger seat and was hit by the smell of new car. It was automatic, so I switched on the engine, revved it up and threw the stick into 'DRIVE' and the motor took off with a rattle of dirt under the bodywork as I screeched across the grass and bumped down on to Clapham Common South Side, and headed towards town and away from trouble.

Or into more.

74

As I drove along Clapham High Street, an ambulance passed me going in the opposite direction towards the common. Poor old Robber. Every time he helped me out he ended up in A & E.

I hoped he was going to be OK.

I looked at Robber's mobile, expecting it to ring at any moment, when the battery indicator started flashing and the light that illuminated the tiny screen went dim, then blinked out altogether, letting me know just at the wrong moment, that my communication system was down.

'Shit, shit, shit!' I yelled, banging on the steering wheel with my fist. God, was Judith all right? Would I ever see her alive again? Where was the Darkman? What the bloody hell was going on? And where could I go?

Soon the car I was driving would be the hottest ticket in town, and I was alone again.

For something to do, I headed for Deptford once more through the snow that was still slowly falling. When I got to Darkman's flat, it was just as Harold, Robber and I had left it, the door still slightly ajar and no one inside. I was amazed. I would've imagined that the local scallywags would've been through it like a bad curry if they'd seen it open and deserted for so long. Perhaps the big black guy had been right: no one messed with the Darkman's stuff. Even when he wasn't around. I found a half-full bottle of Scotch in the living room and drank straight from the neck, and went back into the coke again for company. The flat was cold and I was pissed off. I lit a cigarette and thought that I was about as far up shit creek, paddleless, as I'd ever been in my not particularly illustrious career.

And I missed Judith. And Laura. And another woman who'd been dead for too long and whose pretty face I'd never see again, or hear her silly, beautiful laugh as it tickled my back when we lay in bed together. And I missed a tiny baby girl I'd only seen once, after she'd been cut out of her mother's womb after they'd both burnt to death.

I went looking for the Rover 600 I'd got from Charlie and left parked up outside Darkman's block. Miraculously it was still there in one piece and started on the button. At least that took care of the transport problems. Whilst I let the engine warm up to drive the heater, I sat and had a think.

There was only one place I could go where I might pick up a clue.

So I headed again for the whorehouse in Maida Vale.

75

I got there around seven-thirty and stashed the Rover at the back of a block of flats on the next street. I didn't want to park it out front in case I had to beat a hasty retreat and someone spotted the number. There were signs everywhere about illegally parked cars being clamped. But I didn't think they'd be working that late on Christmas Eve. And if they were, I'd just have to hijack another motor. Ho-hum. All in a day's work.

I walked round to the house and buzzed on the entryphone. As I stood and waited, I turned my collar to the cold and damp and watched the thin coating of snow that lay on the streets being blown into tiny drifts against the front walls.

After a minute I buzzed again, and with a click a female voice answered. 'It's Christmas Eve, we're closed,' she said.

'Is that May?' I said.

'No. It's Emily.'

The Chinese girl.

'Hi, Emily,' I said. 'Is May there?'

'Yes.'

'Get her for me, will you?'

'We're still closed.'

'Get her please, dear.' I was getting bored. And colder by the minute.

I stood there for another thirty seconds before another voice came on and I recognized May's Liverpool accent. 'We're closed,' she said. 'Even we need a break at Christmas.'

'That's what I'm looking for too, May,' I replied, 'a break. It's Nick Sharman.'

There was a pause. 'Oh, it's you,' she said, and she didn't sound overjoyed.

'Well it ain't Father Christmas,' I said. 'Otherwise I'd've just popped down the chimney.'

'What do you want?' she asked.

'To come in. I need somewhere to get my head together for a bit. And you might be able to help me.'

'With what?'

'Just let me in, May. It's freezing out here and it's not something to be discussed on the doorstep.'

'I could just call the police.'

'I'm sure you could. And I'm sure you've got friends on the force. But if you don't let me in I'll just shoot the door down. And your door next. Now that's something that even *your* pals couldn't cover up. Questions would be asked. And there's all that dope you keep around the place. All I want is a bit of a warm, a drink and a little chat. Then I'll be gone and no one ever the wiser. Come on, May. Play the game.'

There was another pause. 'OK,' she said. 'Come on up.' And she buzzed me in.

76

When I got to the flat door, May was waiting. She was covered neck to toe in a scruffy tartan dressing gown, and her hair was in curlers. There was no sign of the heavy who'd sat beside the door previously. 'This is very inconvenient,' she said, as she stepped aside to let me in.

'I know,' I said. 'I just . . .'

'Needed somewhere to lay your weary head,' she interrupted.

'Precisely.'

'Go into the bar.'

'Who's here?'

'Just Emily and me. Now go into the bar.'

I did as she said. I was bone-tired and it was beautifully warm inside the flat. I slumped into one of the armchairs, dropping next to it the case of drugs I'd brought with me from the car. Emily was sitting on one of the stools. She was wearing a dressing gown too, but it was infinitely briefer than May's. And no curlers. A real girls' night in. She gave me a smile when I walked in. The TV was on with the sound turned down. There was a cop show on, featuring a ridiculously handsome young private investigator from south London who never had any trouble solving *his* cases. And always got off with a beautiful woman as he did it.

I envied him.

'Drink?' said May.

'I thought you'd never ask. Beer, please.'

'Emily,' she said.

Emily got me a Beck's and went back to her seat. It tasted like heaven, and I lit a cigarette.

'Annette's not here,' said May. 'I told you, it's just Emily and me.'

'It wasn't Annette I came to see.'

Emily seemed to brighten up at that.

'It was you, May,' I said.

Emily pouted.

May didn't. 'What about?' she said.

'I need to get hold of Darkman.'

'Why?'

197

'He's got my daughter.'

She pondered on that for a moment. 'What for?'

'Long story. I've been to his place. Twice, in fact. No one's home. I thought you might be able to contact him.'

'I might.'

'Will you?'

'What's it worth?'

'It's worth the life of my daughter. And twenty years inside for me as well. I didn't do what the cops think I did. There's people out there know it. Darkman included. But my daughter's the most important. She's only fifteen, May. She's a good girl. Never hurt anyone in her life. Her mum died a few days ago in a plane crash. And now she's been kidnapped. For Christ's sake, if you know how to get hold of Darkman, do it.'

She seemed on the point of refusing. 'Please,' I said.

'I'll make a call,' she said.

77

May used the pay phone in the bar. I wanted her close by when she made the call. Just in case she tried to get clever. She let me hear the engaged tone. I told her to kill the phone. 'I'll try again later,' she said. 'He likes to talk.'

'Tell me about it,' I said.

She called again every quarter of an hour. The number was permanently engaged and I got more and more jumpy. Apart from that, it was quite a pleasant evening. The three of us sat by the bar drinking and smoking and getting quite chummy, like old pals. Emily kept letting her dressing gown slip, and by the end I hadn't seen much more of her than her gynaecologist would. But I wasn't interested. And even old May flashed a bit of leg under her tartan passion killer.

At ten I watched the news. The shoot-out was featured on *London Tonight*. Harold hadn't made it. It was his own stupid fault. Robber was in police custody, although they didn't divulge his name.

Finally, at almost midnight, May tried the number again and said, 'It's ringing.'

I grabbed the phone as it was answered and recognized Darkman's voice. 'Where's my daughter?' I demanded.

'How'd you get this number?'

'Friends in high places.'

'I've been trying to call you, but your phone's switched off.'

'Flat battery. Where's Judith?'

'That was a very stupid thing you did earlier.'

'It wasn't my idea. It was Harold. You know him?'

'Of course.'

'Send flowers. Your driver killed him.'

'Tough.'

'Mr B. won't be pleased.'

'He'll get over it.'

'What about Judith? Is she all right?'

'Yes. You still have the stuff?'

'With me.'

'Good.'

'Let me speak to her.'

There was the usual pause, then I heard Judith's voice. 'Are you all right, Daddy?' she asked.

'Just fine. How about you?'

'I'll be OK. I was so worried about you!'

'Sorry about the shooting,' I said lamely.

199

'You didn't start it. Is your friend hurt badly?'

'I don't know. I hope not.' I didn't want to think about it.

'He wants to talk to you again,' said Judith.

Darkman came back on. 'Satisfied?' he said.

'Yes.'

'Right. I've got a lock-up under the railway arches in Neate Street, Walworth. I've got some things to do right now. Meet me there at three, tomorrow morning. And no tricks. I'm getting tired of all this, Sharman. Your girl's been all right up to now. But my patience is wearing thin. Come alone and bring the stuff.'

And he hung up.

78

Christmas morning

'Is she all right?' asked May when I put down the phone.

'Yes,' I replied. 'All things considered.'

'Good.'

'Listen, May. I've got to impose on your hospitality for a little longer. Sorry.'

'That's not a problem. It's been fun.' Outside, a church clock chimed twelve. 'It's midnight,' she said. 'Christmas Day. Merry Christmas Nick, Emily!'

'Merry Christmas,' I said, though I thought it had never been less merry. And I didn't feel like pulling a cracker.

May gave me a kiss and so did Emily. The latter tried to turn it into something more passionate but I turned my head away. She started to sulk then, and flounced off to bed. May kept me company with a bottle of Scotch and a late film about Santa losing his reindeers, and fell asleep in one of the chairs.

Around two-twenty I split without waking her, went and rescued the car, which hadn't been clamped, and drove south.

Neate Street, London, SE, three o'clock in the morning on Christmas Day. A street that rhymed at 3 a.m. Could be the title for a song.

No one lived on Neate Street. There wasn't a house or block of flats along its half-mile length. It was just a road that led nowhere, and it reminded me of my life.

The main line from Kent to Waterloo ran along one side, high on an embankment over railway arches made from brick that had long ago blackened in the acid south London air. On the other side was a scrubby park that disappeared into the night. There were four street lamps dotted along that side of the road, and one sputtered and fizzed like it would give up the ghost any moment. That was the only sound I heard, apart from my own footsteps and heartbeat as I walked round the corner carrying the case of dope.

I'd parked on the cross street at the bottom, and snorted what felt like half of Bolivia to give myself courage. It wasn't such a good idea, really, as I saw blood on the back of my hand when I touched my nose. All I needed right then was for my sinuses to haemorrhage. As it was, I knew my tongue was swollen and white and I'd chewed the inside of my mouth to a bloody mush.

The clouds were still low, and snow had started fluttering from the sky again in huge flakes that burst on the wet tarmac as they landed. Neate Street waited for me like I was the last living man on the planet, and I drew the Detonics .45 to give myself some courage.

I walked down the pavement opposite the railway arches, looking for some signs of life but seeing none. Not even a stray cat, or a rat looking for supper in the garbage that had collected in the gutters.

Most of the few cars parked at the kerb were wrecks. Burnt-out hulks that had once been someone's pride and joy. But as I passed the second street light I saw, parked across the road between an old Transit and a half-empty skip, Darkman's Mercedes 190 with the black windows.

I crossed the road slowly, fanning the gun as I went, waiting for an ambush but none came. The night was as silent as any night in London could be.

The door to one of the arches was open a crack and I touched it with the toe of my boot. It swung open, revealing a black hole.

I stood outside for a moment waiting and listening. Inside the arch all was silent, but I knew that if I stepped inside I would be silhouetted against the street, making a perfect target for anyone waiting.

But something had to give and in the end it was me. I jumped over the threshold and slid down the wall inside, trying to make myself as small as possible.

Still nothing, but even in the dank atmosphere of the arch I could make out another smell. A smell I had come to know well. The smell of recently fired guns and the newly deceased.

Shit, I thought, I should've brought a torch, and I wished for Robber's company. He always thought of things like that.

I crouched where I was for a moment more, but I could feel no sign of life in the place and hauled out my Zippo and fired it up. In its flickering light I saw the Ford Scorpio parked inside, with bullet holes drilled neatly in the boot. I looked past it and saw the shape of a man's shoe by one of the front tyres. I crabbed round the car for a closer look. The shoe was attached to the body of Darkman's minder, the driver. He was very dead, his leather jacket soaked in blood.

I went back to the door and tried to find a light switch. Eventually I found one and clicked it on. A dim bulb set into the high ceiling came on and I looked round. The minder-driver wasn't the only dead man in the room. Next to him lay the body of the bloke who'd called me on the phone. And propped up against the far wall was Darkman himself, half his head shot away.

Of Judith there was no sign.

79

For fuck's sake, not again, I thought as I looked at the carnage. Where the hell is all this going to end? Then I searched the place. But all that was there, apart from the rubbish accumulated over the years, was the car, a couple of guns that I left where they lay and the three bodies. Three more dead to add to the total. How many was it now? Christ, who could keep count?

Then suddenly I heard a rumbling sound like thunder in the distance that got louder and louder until it seemed as if the whole place would shake apart, and powdery dust from the roof began to drift down to coat the living and the dead. It was like the end of the world, and I looked round in panic until I realized what it was. A trainload of empty coaches heading for Waterloo station or the Kent coast to be parked up ready for its Boxing Day passengers, and I relaxed.

But just for a moment.

Judith. Where the hell was she? And was she all right?

And who had killed Darkman and his sidekicks? It could only have been Mr B. and his mob or Tootsie and the boys.

What a choice.

But I still had the dope. wearily I put the case up on the bonnet of the Scorpio, opened it and dipped into the open packet that was leaking cocaine all over the leather lining. Here goes fuck all, I thought as I lifted my fingers to my nose and scarfed up a good quarter-gram. Here goes my entry ticket to a little rubber room, a straitjacket and lots of cartoons on the TV.

I coughed and spat, and there was blood in my saliva too. But it was too late to worry about things like that.

Then I mentally flipped a coin for where to go next, and came down with Mr B. He was the lesser of the two evils and I prayed that it was him behind all this.

But I had a horrible feeling I was wrong.

80

I went to leave then, to go back to my car. But when I got outside I saw the Merc again and decided that it was a better option than the Rover. I went back inside and checked Darkman's driver's pockets, trying to ignore the blood and stink of him. I found a keyring with a Mercedes badge on it in his jacket pocket.

I went back out to the motor and got in. It started first time and the tank was full, so I put it into gear, pulled away and headed towards Brixton for what I knew, one way or the other, was going to be the last time. You must be crazy, I thought as I drove through the dark, deserted streets. Or have the biggest death wish on the bloody planet.

I arrived at Mr B.'s place at about three-forty-five and it was all lit up like a Christmas tree, which was appropriate for the day, if not for the mood I was in.

I stashed the motor, the dope and my guns out of the way and walked up the path, and the security lights hit me full in the face. I knocked on the front door and waited. After a minute the door cracked and I saw Goldie. Only now he wasn't smiling and showing off his hampsteads, and he held a cocked Browning Hi-Power in his fist. 'The boss is waiting,' he said.

'I hope I haven't got him up.'

'There's no sleep for us souls tonight.'

'Some souls are sleeping permanent.'

He let me in and took me down to Mr B.'s office where Marcus was sitting opposite the big man. 'Darkman's dead,' I said. 'And his men. And my daughter's still missing. But maybe you know about all that.' At least I hoped he did.

He shook his head. 'No,' he said. 'Darkman too? Well, he was looking for it. It was only a matter of time.'

'Shit,' I said.

'Did you think she was here?' he asked.

'I hoped so.'

'How many times do I have to explain that we're not murderers and child snatchers?'

'Only until I believe you.'

'She's not here, I can guarantee you that. Why would I bother to lie?'

'So she's with Tootsie?' I said.

'Yes. He's already been on the phone. He wants that dope, and is ready to do a deal.'

'With you?'

'With whoever's got it.'

'Me.'

'That stuff still belongs to me!'

'But you haven't got it.'

'But I've got you.'

'For how long, this time?'

'As long as I want.'

'I don't think so. I came back voluntarily. You know what happened to Harold?'

'Yes.'

'It was his own fault.'

'He always was impulsive.'

'Messed up my car, too,' said Marcus.

'I'm so sorry,' I said.

'So what do you intend to do?' asked Mr B.

'I intend getting my daughter back.'

'You're looking to be killed then,' said Mr B.

'Not if you send a few of yours with me.'

'Why should my boys get involved?' asked Mr B.

'To clear out Tootsie's rat's nest.'

'You are very optimistic, Mr Sharman,' he said.

'It's a good opportunity for you to come out as top dog,' I said.

'I am top dog.'

'Not as long as Tootsie's in business. You've told me before he's a thorn in your side.'

'A thorn you might well remove for me.'

'So you're going to let me go?'

'Maybe.'

'I'd do better with some help. Someone to watch my back.'

'Marcus?' said Mr B. to his new number two. 'What do you think?'

'I think it's Christmas, and I want to live to enjoy some turkey and yams.'

'You scared, Marcus?' I asked.

'Don't fuck with me, mon,' said Marcus. 'You know I ain't scared, bumble *claat*.'

But I saw his eyes glisten in the near dark of the room and I knew I was close.

'Harold wasn't scared,' I said. 'He was a bloody nuisance, but at least he had some bollocks, even though it cost him his life. But you're scared. Shit scared.' I laughed and gave him the most scathing look I was capable of. 'Of fat old Tootsie and a few scumbags.' Then I changed the subject. 'You got any kids Marcus? Got a babymother stashed away somewhere with a little nipper like Harold did?' I asked him.

'No.'

'You amaze me. I thought you'd've been putting it about all round the manor. Got bad sperm there, son?'

'Shut the fuck up, *raas*.'

'So you don't know what it's like to have a child? A child nicked by those bastards. I hope you do one day and no one's prepared to help you get it back. Motherfucker! What do you say then, Mr B.? Fancy taking out the opposition in one fell swoop? Or are you going to let your hired help call the shots?'

'It's tempting.'

'But the soldiers are chicken.'

'They'll do what I say.'

'Then say it.'

He pondered, but not for long. 'OK, Mr Sharman,' he said. 'You've got yourself an army.'

Thank fuck for that, I thought.

81

'Go get Majesty. Tell him to get the car round. You've got business to attend to. And take Goldie with you,' said Mr B. to Marcus.

'Majesty sleepin',' said Marcus sullenly.

'Then wake him up.'

Marcus gave me a dirty look and left the room.

'They'll be OK,' said Mr B. 'Once they get going.'

'I'm obliged,' I said.

'Don't thank me yet. You haven't got your daughter back. And you were right. I should've taken care of Tootsie long ago.'

'What about the package?'

'Where is it?'

'In my car, just down the road.'

'Take it with you. It might be your only way in. But give it to Marcus to mind.'

'OK,' I said. 'And thanks again.'

Marcus came back five minutes later wearing a long coat and carrying a sawn-off, semi-automatic Winchester shotgun. 'Majesty up,' he said. 'But he not happy.'

'Then make him happy, Marcus,' said Mr B. 'Give him a line. And Mr Sharman here is going to give you the drugs to look after. Don't lose them.'

'Sure,' said Marcus. Then to me. 'Come,' and we left Mr B. to his darkness and his fish and went back to the front of the house where Majesty was still rubbing the sleep from his eyes and Goldie, wearing a natty red duffle coat, was pushing shells into the breech of another Winchester, the twin of the one in Marcus's mitten.

'What you got?' Goldie said to me.

'I've got some handguns in the car,' I replied.

'Want something 'eavy?'

'What you got?'

'Have this,' he said, and tossed me the loaded shotgun. 'Me got somethin' special.' And he pulled back the skirt of his coat to let me see an Uzi carbine in a holster on a leather belt buckled round his waist.

'Get the car, Majesty,' said Marcus. 'Don't keep us mens waitin'.'

'Gimme a livener,' said Majesty, 'me tired.' And Marcus took out a wrap of coke and passed it over. Majesty hoovered up a noseful and passed it to me. I took a hit and gave it to Goldie, who seemed to be the only one of us in a good mood, and he did the same then returned it to Marcus. Marcus ran the paper under his nose, screwed it up and dropped it into his pocket.

'Where's the stuff?' Marcus said to me.

'I'll get it. Wait here.'

I handed Goldie the shotgun, left them in the hall and went back to the Merc. I stashed the four guns I'd collected about my person and took the bag back to the house, where I gave it to Marcus. 'Let's fuckin' go,' he said. 'It's gettin' late.'

We went out into the night which seemed to be getting colder, but at least the snow had stopped. Majesty led us to another Beemer which was parked in front of the next house, activated the central locking and we got in. Me in the back with Goldie, Majesty behind the wheel and Marcus riding shotgun. Literally.

Majesty hit the ignition, switched on the lights and headed for Loughborough Junction.

The streets were empty and he drove like a maniac, chucking the car round corners and jumping red lights like they didn't exist. I don't know if it was the coke, or being dragged out of bed, or the excitement at what was happening, or just that he was a fucking flake, but about a quarter of a mile from Loughborough Junction station, he underestimated the sharpness of a bend or maybe hit a sheet of black ice just as he went into it. Whatever. It doesn't matter now. All I know was that the BMW spun out, Majesty hit the brakes too hard, the motor's wheels clipped the kerb and suddenly we were rolling down the middle of the road, the engine still roaring, and sparks flying from the bodywork each time the car turned turtle. The door next to me flew open, snapped off its hinges and I was thrown across the pavement on my back, still clutching the Winchester, as the car skidded along on its roof and hit a lamp-post with a crash. I lay on the ground and saw petrol ignite before the car went up with a whoosh, and the last thing I saw was Marcus hanging down by his seat belt, his hands flailing at the catch, before he was consumed by flames. And the last thing I heard was the screams of the occupants of the BMW as they burnt to death, a sound I don't think I'll ever forget as long as I live.

82

Then the ammunition that was in the guns and on their persons began to go off like a firework display, and I knew it was time to split. Shit, I thought as I limped away from the blazing motor, and realized that the bag of dope was still inside and had gone up with the car and its occupants. That's put a spanner in the works.

I headed through the back streets towards the Loughborough Estate and Tootsie's place, as lights came on in windows at the racket, and I knew the coppers wouldn't be long arriving. Well, at least they had something to keep them busy and out of my hair.

Once I was away from all the commotion, I stopped, leaned against a wall, lit a cigarette with trembling fingers and assessed the damage to my person. I was getting too old for this lark.

My jeans were ripped at the knee and I could feel blood trickling down one leg; my leather jacket was torn at the shoulder, the lining exposed, and my back was burning like hell. I tried to lift my left arm but couldn't get it above shoulder level without excruciating pain. It felt like my collarbone was broken.

A fine state in which to go into battle, and single-handed.

What the hell, I thought. Here goes nothing. I flipped the cigarette away and got going, wishing I had something to drink or another line of coke.

I cut across the estate to the old shop that Tootsie and his crew had squatted and got there at four-forty a.m. by my Rolex that seemed to have survived the crash much better than I had. I was glad I hadn't let those geezers in Vauxhall rip it off.

The shop was in darkness, as was the whole parade. Obviously Tootsie and his mob had been target-practising on the street lights again.

Good boys, I thought as I slid like a wraith through the shadowy walkways towards my objective.

The graffiti-covered shutters were down at the front so I went round to the alley at the back, just as it started to snow again.

The service doors were blocked by an overflowing skip. Shit, I thought, and looked up. The windows above were filthy, but they looked like they were free of security measures, and beyond one I could just see a dim light. That looked like a decent mode of entry, so I pumped a shell into the breech of the Winchester and went a-hunting.

I walked back along the alley to a wooden door at the end. It was warped and stained with smoke and gave slightly when I pushed it, although it nearly killed my sore back to exert much pressure.

I leaned all my weight against it and felt it give again, then give more, and with a screech it opened a foot or so.

I froze, waiting for reaction to the sound, but none came and I slid through the gap.

Inside was a foul-smelling, pitch-black hole that I illuminated briefly with my lighter, and saw a stairway leading upwards.

Moving by touch, I took the stairs which dog-legged after eight steps and after another eight ended at a landing. I lit the Zippo again and saw a black-painted window to my left. It was the direction I wanted. I tried it but it was stuck fast.

I lifted up the Winchester and hit the glass with the butt,

once gently, the second time harder, and the third time hard enough to break the pane.

The sound of the glass falling on to the balcony outside, that reached the length of the rear of the parade, sounded as loud as an explosion in the still night air, and I reversed the gun and stuck the barrel through the hole.

But still there was no reaction from inside Tootsie's hideout. Either there was no one home, they were all deaf, or they'd been celebrating their victory over Darkman by smoking so much weed and drinking so much booze they were all dead to the world.

I hoped it was the latter.

83

I cleared the frame of glass and pulled myself through, then crept along the balcony, which was inches-deep in filthy water and lichen and all sorts of other shit, and stank like a midden when I disturbed the crust of ice that covered it.

When I got to the window that was lit, I peered through, taking care not to silhouette my head against the outside. The interior light came from an open doorway, but as far as I could see, the room inside was empty. I tried the window but it wouldn't budge. It was either locked or stuck with old paint. I had two choices, either smash it, which would alert anyone inside, no matter how fast asleep they were, or try the stealthy approach.

I decided on stealth.

Stiffly I lay down in the icy water outside the window and, with the barrel of the pump, I tapped on the glass above me.

Nothing.

Fuck, but it was cold, as I lay shivering in the muck and the freezing water permeated my clothing.

A harder tap.

Still nothing, and I'd half decided to smash the window anyway when I saw the light brighten suddenly, then decrease again as someone approached the dirty glass, throwing a slight shadow over me. I snuggled – if that's the word – against the brickwork as the window opened with a squeal and a black head stuck itself through. It was Clarence. I put the muzzle of the gun under his chin and said. 'Season's greetings, Clarence.'

'Wha'?' he stuttered.

'Is my daughter there?'

The bastard was quick, I'll give him that. He withdrew his head and the window went down with a slam.

I'll take that as a yes, I thought, pulled myself upright and fired through the glass. The window disintegrated and Clarence took the blast full in his back and somersaulted against the wall.

So much for the stealthy approach.

84

I pumped another shell into the breech, then cleared the shards of glass away with the barrel of the gun and climbed into the room. Clarence's body was still, and so was the rest of the building. I stopped at the door and listened. Not a sound.

Now that was weird. The commotion I'd made should've brought the boys running, semi-automatic weapons cocked and unlocked.

I stood in the doorway for a moment more, every sense primed for trouble, but the whole place stayed perversely silent. I moved slowly into the dimly lit corridor that was strewn with litter and, with my gun pointed in front of me. started to search. I didn't have far to look. The third door I tried revealed a hot, sparsely lit room that stank of dope, sweat and sex, with a mattress on the floor covered in a grubby duvet next to one of those big Calor-gas heaters. Under the duvet was a young black woman of heroic proportions. 'Where is everybody?' I said, by way of starting a conversation.

'What's happening?' she replied. 'Where's Clarence?'

'Your boyfriend?' I asked back.

'No. Just a guy I met.'

'Just as well. He's dead. Where's Tootsie and the rest?'

'Who?'

'Tootsie. Big fat geezer. Clarence's boss man.'

'Don't know. There's nobody here but us chickens.' And she giggled a stoned giggle.

'So where are they?'

'Find out.'

I knelt on the edge of the mattress right up close until I almost gagged at her body odour. If that bitch had washed her cunt in the last week I'd've been amazed. I changed the shotgun over to my left hand and stuck the muzzle up into the folds of her triple chins and said, 'I will. Don't worry about that. Was there a young white girl here?'

She sniggered, so I hit her so hard with my right fist that her head bounced on the wall and blood dribbled from the

215

side of her mouth. 'Don't fuck with me, darling,' I said. 'I'm not in the mood. Believe me, I'm not. You said it yourself: there's no one here but us chickens, and I can blow your head to shit with just one touch of my finger. I killed the other geezer in there and it won't worry me to make it a brace of schwartzers tonight.'

'She was here,' she said, wiping her blood away with the back of her hand and allowing the duvet to drop, showing me her massive breasts.

'Where is she now?'

'Tootsie took her.'

'Where?'

'His place in Kennington.'

Shit, I thought, and I've got no motor again.

'Alone?' I asked.

'With Ramon.'

'Have they hurt her?'

'Not yet.'

I felt a cold hand clutch at my heart again. If anyone touched Judith they were dead meat. But that could never replace what they'd taken from her.

'Did Clarence have a car?' I asked.

'Yeah. A Shogun.'

'Where?'

'Parked down the road by the telephone box.'

'Keys?'

She pointed her hand at a jacket that was draped over a wooden chair in the corner of the room. Clarence's, I imagined, and I picked it up and patted the pockets until I found a set of ignition keys on a Playboy keyring. 'Good,' I said. 'Now what do I do with you?'

'I won't do anything.'

216

'Is that right?'

She nodded. 'And you can have me if you want.'

'No thanks,' I said, looking at her obese body which she was doing nothing to hide. 'I've given up pork.'

'Bastard.'

'That's more like it. Seems to me I can trust you, tie you, or kill you.'

Her face took on a greyish hue and she pulled the duvet over her body again.

'I don't want to kill you,' I said. 'But you've seen me now, and I killed your boyfriend.'

'I told you, he's not my boyfriend, just a john. A trick.'

'OK,' I said. 'But I'll have to tie you up.'

She seemed a bit more cheerful then. 'Is that how you get your kicks?' she asked, with what I imagined she thought was a coquettish smile.

'No,' I said. 'But I don't want you warning Tootsie I'm about.'

'I wouldn't.'

'Even so,' and I looked around for something with which to truss her up tight. As my eyes left her she came off the bed with a cut-throat razor in her hand and slashed at me. The blade went through my leather and dug into my chest, and I felt as if I'd been punched hard. I pulled the trigger on the pump and blew her belly clear through her spinal cord.

She crashed back against the wall and rolled on to her side as I looked at the blood bubbling through the slice in my jacket.

Fuck it, I thought. I should've just killed her anyway.

85

By then I was hurting all over and felt like warmed-up shit. I looked round the room and saw the girl's clothes. On top was a black satin slip that smelled of cheap perfume and sweat. But nevertheless I folded it up and stuffed it down the front of my shirt to try and stop some of the bleeding. This was going to be a great Christmas. It was the casualty ward at King's or the undertaker's for me, for sure, by Boxing Day.

Then I picked up the car keys and split.

The 4×4 was parked just where she'd said it'd be, and I worked the gizmo on the keyring that switched off the alarm and unlocked the doors and climbed in. Thank God it was automatic, because I wasn't up to shifting gears manually. I plugged in the key and fired it up. Someone had fitted a straight-through exhaust, and the sound boomed off the buildings around as I stuck it into 'DRIVE' and took off with a squeal from the motor's oversized tyres.

Even though I took it fairly easy, what with my shoulder and back hurting like fuck, and Christ knows how much blood I was losing from the razor cut, I was in Kennington within ten minutes and parked the motor up about three minutes' walk from Tootsie's gaff there.

I shut down the motor, switched off the lights, lit a last cigarette, picked up the shotgun and went looking for my daughter and the people who'd kidnapped her for what I prayed was the last time.

The house was lit when I got there and a metal cover was on the front door. Christ, I thought, these motherfucking Yardies are keeping the south London welding companies in business. I went round the back and checked the door there. No cover, stupid arseholes. I blew the locks off with one shot, kicked it open and went inside. Ramon was standing in the kitchen in a vest and trousers holding a can of Stripe, and I blew the fucker away and pumped the last shell into the breech of the Winchester.

'Come on out, Tootsie, you motherfucker!' I screamed. 'Come on out and see what I brought you for Christmas!' But answer came there none.

I walked further into the building, kicking open the doors to the living room as I went, before I got to the stairs at the front and climbed them slowly.

At the top I stopped. There was only one light on. A dim, shadeless bulb in a ceiling fixture. I padded across the carpet and pushed open a door that led into the bathroom. It was empty.

I began to turn round and sensed a movement behind me and tried to bring up the gun, but suddenly the dim bulb became as bright as the sun, then as dark as the night, and I fell into a black, warm sea of unconsciousness.

86

I came to lying on a hard floor. My hands were tied behind my back, and if I thought I was hurting before, now I was certain. Every sodding bone and tissue in my body was telegraphing pain to my brain. And on top of that I felt as if someone had taken a can-opener to my skull.

I groaned aloud and opened my eyes. I was in a small

bedroom. It was furnished with a single divan, a wardrobe, a dressing table and the walls were covered with posters of Bob Marley, Snoop Doggy Dog and Ice T. Judith was kneeling over me and Tootsie was standing in the doorway, a Hi-Power in his fist, and my Detonics tucked into the waistband of his trousers. The other three of my guns were littered on the top of the dressing table, well out of my reach.

'Are you all right, Dad?' Judith sounded worried. 'I thought you were never going to wake up.'

'As well as can be expected. What's more important, how are you? Have they hurt you?'

'The other one kept touching me.'

'Don't worry about him,' I said. 'I've sorted him. Did he . . . ?'

'Shut up,' interrupted Tootsie, his massive jowls wobbling.

'No,' said Judith. 'I bit him.'

'Good for you,' I said. 'But you might have poisoned yourself.'

'I said shut up both of you,' ordered Tootsie, his voice climbing an octave. 'And you, bitch, get away from him, back on the bed.'

'Don't call her a bitch, Tootsie,' I said. 'She'd make two of you, gross as you are.'

'Shut up, Sharman,' said Tootsie, who came over, grabbed Judith by the hair and slung her on to the divan, then stood over me.

'You're a dead man for that, Tootsie,' I said as calmly as I could under the circumstances, and a lot more bravely than I felt. 'Dead meat, fat boy.'

He cocked the pistol. 'Don't be stupid, man. You're in no position to threaten me.'

And I wasn't. And all three of us knew it.

'No, man,' he went on. 'You're the one who's going to die. You killed my man, Ramon.'

'And Clarence at the other place,' I said. 'And his tart. She was a fat whore. Relation of yours, was she?'

Tootsie's nostrils flared and he kicked me in the side. Just one more little pain to add to the whole.

'Where's the dope, Sharman?' he demanded.

'The dope,' I said. 'The McGuffin. The whole point of this fucking exercise. It's gone, mate. All gone. All burnt up with three of Mr B.'s finest in a car crash down Loughborough Junction way. Just ashes.'

'You're lying.'

'*Au contraire,* Tootsie,' I said. 'I speak nothing but the truth. The driver missed a bend and the car was wrecked. Look at the state of me, man. That happened when I was thrown clear. The others all died. Cooked. But then you're used to watching people crash and burn, aren't you, fat man? Look at what happened to that plane in Chicago. The plane that Judith's mother and stepfather and little baby brother were on. It was your mates that blew those poor bleeders out of the sky, wasn't it?'

Judith's head snapped round at my words.

'Yeah, man,' said Tootsie. 'Sure it was. You knew that already. Now forget that shit. Are you telling the truth about the dope?'

'Yeah,' I said, tired. I was fed up by then. What was the point of going on? It was only a matter of time before he finished me off, and maybe that would be for the best. Except for Judith, of course. I looked at her and tried to get something of how sorry I was in the look.

'Sucker,' said Tootsie, raising the pistol until I looked down its deadly black bore. 'You should've lied. Now there's no point in keeping you alive. Get ready to meet your maker.'

'No!' said Judith. 'Don't you hurt him.' And she came off the bed, grabbed Robber's .44 magnum from where Tootsie had left it on the dressing table and held it in both hands, pointing at Tootsie.

87

Tootsie froze, then swivelled his bloodshot eyes in Judith's direction until he finally turned his massive head to look at her. But the Hi-Power was still aimed at my chest and his finger was still hard on the trigger. But for the first time I sensed real fear in the man.

'Well, little miss,' he said in an oily voice. 'That was clever. I knew I should've kept you tied up.'

'Put the gun down,' said Judith. 'Or I'll shoot you.'

Tootsie laughed a forced laugh. 'You ain't gonna shoot no one, little lady. The safety catch is on.'

'There's no safety catch on a revolver,' said Judith authoritatively, and as if to prove the point, she cocked the hammer with an oily click.

Tootsie twitched, so did his trigger finger, so did I.

'Put the gun down,' said Judith again.

Tootsie shook his head. 'No, no, no,' he said. 'No little girl's going to get the better of me. I just don't figure you've got the stuff to pull that trigger. You're shaking already.'

And he was right, she was. Little quivers going all through her body and hands, and the gun.

'I've got the stuff,' said Judith, but her voice broke as she said it and Tootsie smiled evilly.

I kept quiet. This was between the pair of them.

Judith licked her lips, but her face was determined. 'I mean it.'

'Like hell,' said Tootsie, and started to bring the Browning round in her direction. Time seemed to slow and I saw Judith's face as she was as a baby and as a little girl and how she would be as a grown woman. And I wanted to scream, but my throat was frozen, and still the Browning turned, and I saw Judith's finger whiten on the trigger of the Smith. 'You killed my mummy!' she screamed, and the hammer went down on the cartridge and then everything sped up again.

The first bullet took Tootsie in the side, and the recoil of the massive gun slammed Judith back against the wall. But Tootsie kept on turning the Hi-Power and Judith fired again, but the second bullet missed him altogether and chopped plaster from the wall. Then she fired again for the third and last time, and the slug hit him just under his jaw and blew the back of his head off, and he fell on to the carpet at my feet with a thud that shook the house.

'Citizen's arrest, motherfucker,' I said to myself.

Judith dropped the gun and I saw tears in her eyes as she came to me and put her arms around me.

'Nice shooting, sweetheart,' I said. 'But I think you'd better untie me now.'